BEACON STREET GIRLS

This book belongs to:

VERITAS AMICITIA GAUDIUM
truth friendship fun!

™

BEACON STREET GIRLS

Be sure to read all of our books:

BSG Special Adventure Books:

Coming soon:

BEACON STREET GIRLS®

Just Kidding

BY
ANNIE BRYANT

ALADDIN MIX

NEW YORK LONDON TORONTO SYDNEY

We'd like to thank the experts who helped make *Just Kidding* possible, including: Rachel Simmons, the author of the *New York Times* bestseller *Odd Girl Out: The Hidden Culture of Aggression in Girls*; Rob Nickel, president, Kid Innovation Canada; the Internet Keep Safe Coalition, a non-profit organization dedicated to giving parents, educators, and caregivers the information and tools that empower them to teach children the safe and healthy use of technology and the Internet; and Katelyn M. LeClerc, the Internet Safety Program Coordinator, Office of the Attorney General of Massachusetts.

ALADDIN MIX
An imprint of Simon & Schuster Children's Publishing Division
1230 Avenue of the Americas, New York, NY 10020

Designed by Dina Barsky
Manufactured in the United States of America
First Aladdin MIX edition July 2009
2 4 6 8 10 9 7 5 3 1
Library of Congress Control Number 2008935909
ISBN: 978-1-4169-6440-7

Who's Who

BSG

Katani Summers
aka Kgirl . . . Katani has a strong fashion sense and business savvy. She is stylish, loyal & cool.

Avery Madden
Avery is passionate about all sports and animal rights. She is energetic, optimistic & outspoken.

Charlotte Ramsey
A self-acknowledged "klutz" and an aspiring writer, Charlotte is all too familiar with being the new kid in town. She is intelligent, worldly & curious.

Isabel Martinez
Her ambition is to be an artist. She was the last to join the Beacon Street Girls. She is artistic, sensitive & kind.

Maeve Kaplan-Taylor
Maeve wants to be a movie star. Bubbly and upbeat, she wears her heart on her sleeve. She is entertaining, friendly & fun.

Ms. Razzberry Pink
The stylishly pink proprietor of the Think Pink boutique is chic, gracious & charming.

Marty
The adopted best dog friend of the Beacon Street Girls is feisty, cuddly & suave.

Happy Lucky Thingy and alter ego **Mad Nasty Thingy** Marty's favorite chew toy, it is known to reveal its alter ego when shaken too roughly. He is most often happy.

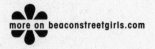

more on beaconstreetgirls.com

Part One
The Break-up Heard 'Round the World

1

The Late, Great Maeve Kaplan-Taylor

Maeve scrunched up her favorite puffy pillow and rolled over. Suddenly, something seemed strange . . . very strange. Sunlight was peeking through the sides of the curtains and making funny lines on her bedspread, but the clock said 4:07 a.m. Since when was it ever sunny at 4 o'clock in the morning?

Maeve grabbed her pink leather watch off the nightstand and stared at the digital numbers. Her eyes widened. 8:20 a.m.! That couldn't be right! School would be starting in ten minutes. Normally slow-moving in the morning, Maeve shot out of bed. Her bedroom, the pink palace, was in chaos . . . books and clothes scattered everywhere. "Ouch!" she screamed as she stubbed her toe on the nightstand. Where was everybody?

"MOM!" Maeve shrieked. "I am soooo late! Where *are* you?" She began riffling through an abominably messy pile of just-washed clothes. She finally found her favorite pair of jeans. Wiggling into them at super speed, she moaned out loud. Her guinea pigs, recently renamed Flora and Fauna, squeaked for some snacks. Maeve stumbled over to their cage and tossed in some fresh guinea pig pellets. "Flora and Fauna, I just *have* to get more organized," she said as she gave them a scratch behind the ears.

Maeve heard a door swing open and quick footsteps in the hallway. "Oh, no!" cried her mother. "The power must have gone out! I'm going to jump in the shower. Maeve, Sam, get up, fast as you can!" Ms. Kaplan yelled down the hallway.

Maeve threw on a pink cable-knit sweater over her fitted white T. She furiously laced up her sneakers and bounced over to the mirror to scrunch gel into her mass of red curls. She spritzed body spray into the air and twirled into the mist . . . a trick she learned from her friend Katani's older sister Patrice. "Misting," Patrice said, "is a total fragrance experience." Swinging her book bag over her shoulder, Maeve grabbed her keys and backpack and rushed out of her bedroom, down the hall, and into the kitchen.

Maeve's eight-year-old brother, Sam, was calmly sitting at the kitchen table slurping down a huge bowl of his favorite crunch cereal. He was also reading a comic book and looking as if he didn't have a care in the world. He glanced up as Maeve dropped her bag right in front of him. She stared down at him and tapped her foot.

Then she breathed in deeply and let it out in a slow *whoosh*. Her new yoga instructor, Gail, had taught her the power of deep breathing in stressful situations. "How come you're all ready to go?" Maeve asked Sam, her voice cracking.

"I always set my watch alarm for five minutes after my alarm clock. You know, in case something happens. Like the power goes out, or whatever. I was reading in this magazine that military dudes have to do that because they get in lots of trouble if they are late for—"

"SAM! WHY didn't you wake us up?!" Maeve simply could not believe that Sam was up and didn't wake them. She wanted to scream.

Sam, who looked a little embarrassed, answered, "Well I was going to but I guess I . . . forgot."

"You *forgot*? WHAT—" Maeve was about to give Sam a piece of her mind but he looked so sheepish she stopped. *He's only eight after all.* Sam started reading chapter books when he was five, and he was such a math brainiac that Maeve sometimes forgot he was only in third grade.

"Uh, it's okay," Maeve said generously. "I guess it's not your fault the power went out."

Sam burped and pushed his chair back and brought his dirty dishes to the dishwasher, while Maeve grabbed all three of their brown-bag lunches from the fridge. "You know Sam, you're never going to get a girlfriend if you do gross things like that." Sam grinned and ran out of the room.

Maeve glanced at her watch. "Mom, you better hurry! It's already eight twenty-six!" she shouted up the stairs. Her mom was supposed to be at work at 8:30, and she had to drop Sam off at the elementary school on her way.

Since their apartment was just down the street from Abigail Adams Junior High, Maeve usually walked to school. Today, it was going to have to be a run.

Ms. Kaplan raced down the stairs, cradling her boots in one arm and brushing her hair with the other. Sam came skidding back into the kitchen after her. She glanced at her children and smiled. "Oh good, you're all ready. You kids are quick. Let's get this train moving!"

Maeve's mom grabbed a piece of paper and scribbled a quick note. "Don't worry, hon. Give this to Mrs. Fields if you get caught coming in late."

Maeve grabbed the note and gave her mom a quick hug before grabbing her coat. "See ya!" she called as she raced out the front door, her curls bouncing. Halfway to the crosswalk, Maeve stopped short and dug into her school bag. They were having an open-book social studies test that day, and she had a sinking feeling her textbook was sitting on the desk in her bedroom. "Ughhhh!" Maeve cried out loud. This had to be the most frustrating morning ever. She sprinted back to the apartment for take two.

Panting, Maeve waved to her mother and Sam, who were just getting into the car. "Forgot something!" she called as she swung open the front door. Thankfully, her social studies book was right on her desk. Maeve grabbed it and reversed direction at lightning speed. She pulled the door shut behind her and raced to the crosswalk for the second time in the past thirty seconds.

By the time she got to Abigail Adams Junior High, Maeve could see that the steps were empty and the busses were gone. *Great*, Maeve thought. *Just great. I might as well go to the office and ask for a detention slip!*

As soon as she opened the door to the school building, she knew she was in trouble. There wasn't a single person in the hallways, and everything was unnaturally quiet. Obviously, the bell had already rung. While Maeve loved dramatic entrances, she hated starting off the school day on the wrong foot by being late. It usually meant a whole bunch of terrible things were going to happen . . . like some teacher would be giving a surprise quiz and because you were late you had to take a seat in the back of the room. Or Anna and Joline, aka Queens of Mean, would make some major snide comment about what you were wearing and you would have to say something back. It was so annoying.

At least she had a tardy note. But when she reached into her pocket, she only pulled out her lip gloss. Maeve checked her other pockets, then her school bag, and then frantically did a 360-degree turn to see if the note was somewhere on the floor. She realized with horror that the note was gone. Somehow, somewhere, between the apartment and school, it had disappeared. She just knew it. Everything was going to be a big fat mess today. *Well*, Maeve thought, *there is nothing to do but go back and look for it* . . . otherwise she was tardy without an excuse, punishable by detention . . . and that would make the day a complete disaster. She took another deep yoga breath. *Maybe there is something to this yoga stuff*, she thought as she started to calm down. She was totally against yoga when her mother first suggested it, but when she heard her hip hop instructor say that most dancers practiced yoga before performances, she thought she would give it a try. Now she found herself practicing her yoga postures in her spare time. She had taught Avery a few poses and Avery declared them "very cool." Ave's favorite was "downward dog." Big surprise. Avery loved dogs.

As Maeve started toward the door, she saw Mr. Clauson, the school janitor, toss a big garbage bag he'd obviously just filled outside into the giant trash bin. Maeve realized that there was a good chance her note was somewhere in that pile.

Nope. Maeve shook her head and grimaced. *Yoga or no yoga, there is no way that I am rooting through garbage to find that note! That's simply too much to ask of a movie star in training. Who even knows what else is in there?* Maeve shuddered at the thought. *I'd rather take detention!*

Ms. Rodriguez, her homeroom teacher, was pretty cool about most things. Maeve crossed her fingers and hoped that if she explained how awful the morning had been so far, maybe Ms. R would give her a break. Right now, it was her only chance. She began practicing her speech. "Ms. R it was a total tragedy. The power went off, my mother overslept, and my genius brother was occupied with reading comic books and plotting the destruction of the Western world. . . ."

She was feeling pretty confident when a sudden burst of laughter from the direction of the gym startled her. It was the first sound she'd heard since coming into the building, and she wondered what was going on. Late or not, she just had to check it out. Maeve walked up to the gym door and peered inside, her deep blue eyes widening at what she saw.

To her surprise, there were no students at all in the gym. On the other hand, every teacher in the school was there. Mrs. Fields was handing out oversized T-shirts to each teacher. Maeve scrunched up her eyes and looked closely. Every T-shirt directly related to each teacher's specialty. There was a big trombone on Ms. Ciara's T-shirt—which made sense, since Ms. C taught music. Ms. Rodriguez taught English, so her T-shirt had a big dictionary on the front. Mr. Sherman, who taught pre-algebra and had earned the nickname "The Crow," had on a shirt that said "X + 128 = 150."

Figures, Maeve thought. *He'll probably make me go to the board and solve that problem in class today. Why ruin a good T-shirt with a math problem?* Math was Maeve's worst subject, and the Crow was her least favorite teacher in the world. Nothing he did seemed funny to her. Suddenly, all the teachers clustered around Mrs. Fields and Mr. Lewis, the band director. Mr. Lewis wore a T-shirt over his full band uniform, and he was lightly tapping on a huge bass drum he'd strapped to his chest.

What in the world was going on? It looked like the teachers were getting ready to put on a performance of *The Music Man*! Maeve loved that movie, especially when she was young. She had always nagged her father to run it for her at the Beacon Street Movie House, which he owned. She loved to sing along with Robert Preston and Ron Howard, who was really cute when he was little. Now he was a big-time director. . . .

Suddenly Mrs. Fields blew her whistle. *Oh my gosh!* Maeve put her hand over her mouth. She realized what all this weirdness was *really* about. It had nothing to do with

The Music Man. It was the moment she and her classmates had been waiting for all year. It was finally about to happen, and she, Maeve Kaplan-Taylor, *was the only kid in the entire school who knew it*. She was the star witness.

I am the messenger of totally good tidings, Maeve thought as she sped toward homeroom, clutching her bag. She didn't even want to pause to sling the bag over her shoulder. She had to be the one to break the news. It was just *too* terribly exciting!

"Hey, everybody," she called out as she burst through the door of Ms. R's room. "I have the biggest news! You're not gonna believe it, but it's finally—"

Before she could get the words out, the PA system crackled to life with the sound of the Abigail Adams fight song on full blast.

Maeve joined in the final words of the refrain in her perky soprano voice, "Abigail Adams hearts unite!"

"Students, please take your seats!" Mrs. Fields ordered over the loudspeaker. Maeve plopped into her seat, a huge smile on her face. The principal continued, "The biggest, the baddest, the most spectacular, the most fabulous week at Abigail Adams Junior High is about to begin!"

There was no need for that announcement, because everyone in the classroom could hear the rhythmic thumping of the big bass drum and the parade of teachers marching down the hall. The students sat straight in their seats. More attentive than they usually were at that time of the morning, they waited with shining eyes, listening to the glorious thump of that drum bringing Spirit Week closer and closer to their classroom door.

2

"Be True to Your School"

For a long moment it was completely quiet in the room; Maeve could actually hear her classmates breathing. Then Riley Lee, leader of the band Mustard Monkey, began to tap his pencil lightly on his desk, keeping time with the sound of the bass drum coming closer and closer down the hallway. *Rap, tap* . . . The faces of the other kids broke into grins. That Riley could really drum.

Henry Yurt, who was not only class clown but also, surprisingly, class president, leaped out of his seat. "What we need now is a leader for this band," he declared. In a minute, the Yurtmeister was marching up and down the aisles between desks, high-stepping and swinging his arms hilariously like he was leading a band at halftime. Outside, the class could hear the sounds of laughter and talking as teachers stopped, one by one, at their own classrooms. Unable to resist, Riley jumped up and fell into line behind Henry. In a minute, three or four other boys followed, marching solemnly but with goofy grins up and down the aisles. A few girls joined in and the group formed a conga line. Maeve was one of the girls. She couldn't resist being part of a dance line. Soon she had everyone adding a hip hop rhythm.

Charlotte Ramsey was astounded. Her green eyes were filled with bewilderment. She had lived all over the world with her journalist-father and had seen lots of interesting things, including a leopard chasing a herd of antelopes, but this was definitely a new and unique experience! WHAT was everybody doing?

Charlotte's friend Katani Summers noticed her total confusion. The two girls, along with Maeve, Avery Madden, and Isabel Martinez, were best friends and had formed their own club called the Beacon Street Girls after they met in Ms. R's homeroom at the beginning of the year. Katani, who always wore the hippest outfits, was wearing black dress pants, a long-sleeved purple shirt, and a gorgeous multicolored printed scarf tossed carelessly but artfully over her shoulders. It all looked just too perfect with her gold and topaz earrings and her chic, twisted-up hairstyle. Since she was always so fabulously dressed, Katani might have seemed interested only in fashion, but she was also one of the most organized and serious people Charlotte had ever met. At that moment she grinned at Charlotte's total confusion. "Pretty strange, huh?" Katani whispered.

Charlotte turned to stare at her. "What *is* this?" she whispered back.

Katani grabbed a notepad from her backpack and began writing furiously. Quickly she tore out the paper, which she had emblazoned with her own personal Kgirl logo, folded it, and slipped it to Charlotte.

Charlotte smiled. Only Katani would think to decorate her notepad. She opened the note and read, in Katani's hasty but distinct scrawl: "You have just landed on Planet Spirit, where you must smile nonstop for a week."

Charlotte's eyes got even bigger. "Is that even humanly possible?" she whispered to Katani.

Katani took back the note, crossed out what she had written, and scribbled on it again. When it came back to Charlotte, it read, "Just kidding!" with a huge smiley face.

Charlotte grinned at her friend. "Very funny," she mouthed.

Suddenly, the classroom door swung open. The student marchers dispersed in a single instant, sliding into their seats and sitting up straight as Ms. R entered the room.

Ms. R smiled as she marched in solemnly and sat down at her desk. "It's Spirit Week!" she announced, "and this is what I think of it." She pointed to her oversized T-shirt so the class would read the quote underneath the picture of the dictionary: BE TRUE TO YOUR SCHOOL.

The class burst into cheers and whoops. Henry Yurt pumped his fist in the air and let out a "Yeeeee-haaaaaaw!"

When the noise died down, Dillon Johnson pointed to Ms. R's T-shirt and asked, "Who said that?" Dillon was one of the best athletes in the seventh grade. He sometimes had a crush on Maeve–they had even gone on a sort-of date to a Celtics game–and was usually a pretty good guy.

Right now, though, it looked as though Riley was

going to have a heart attack. He was shaking his head back and forth. Finally, he managed to sputter, "The Beach Boys, man! It's one of their biggest hits! You never heard 'Be True to Your School'? It's like a vintage rock classic. I mean Brian Wilson is a certified genius."

Maeve grinned. Riley was like a one-man rock 'n' roll encyclopedia. Meanwhile, Dillon looked annoyed. He told Riley to chill. "Not everybody knows every rock 'n' roll song ever made."

Ignoring him, Riley began to hum the tune, but Ms. R stopped him gently. "Okay, Riley. Thanks. Everybody get back in your seats. I have to read the rules for Spirit Week so everyone knows what's going to happen."

She picked up a colorful sheet of paper lying on her desk and began to read. "All classes in all periods will be shorter every day this week."

There was an immediate outbreak of applause, led by the twins, Josh and Billy Trentini, and Avery Madden. Avery, the smallest but most athletic of the BSG, loved everything to do with sports. She was often found playing pickup basketball or giving her two cents about the Red Sox to whoever would listen. "I just can't wait until opening day at Fenway," Charlotte heard her telling the guys the other day at lunch. Of course that was months away. Charlotte just hoped her friend could contain herself until then.

Since there was a great deal of head spinning and whispering going on, Ms. R looked up at the class and raised her eyebrows. Even though she was a favorite teacher at Abigail Adams, kids knew that the "eyebrow raise" meant business. The students quieted down, and the teacher read on. "Every student will be asked to sign up for either the dance committee, the sports committee, or the community service committee. We're all going to be working together to make this week special and to do our school proud. The point of Spirit Week is to think about what spirit really means to you. It could be about your feelings for your school, or your community, or your family."

Before she could go further, there was a knock at the classroom door.

When the door opened, all eyes turned.

In walked Kevin Connors, superstar athlete, starring in almost all the school sports events, and current boyfriend of Amanda Cruz, who was the star player for Abigail Adams girls' basketball team. They were like Abigail Adams' movie stars. Even Anna and Joline, pop stars in their own minds, were in awe. Maeve was thrilled. She thought Kevin was dreamy.

"What's Mr. Hotshot doing here?" Katani whispered to Charlotte. Katani didn't have anything against Kevin Connors, but she could never understand why people (her friend Maeve for instance) made such a huge deal out of someone they didn't even know.

Charlotte also wondered why Kevin would walk into Ms. R's class in the middle of homeroom . . . especially with all the Spirit Week craziness going on.

Ms. R heard giggles as some of the girls whispered to each other. She pointedly ignored them. "Oh, Kevin, come on in," she said. "There's an empty seat in the fourth row, next to Julie." She turned to the class. "Kevin will be joining our homeroom," Ms. R announced with a welcoming smile.

"But Ms. Rodriguez," Betsy Fitzgerald spoke as she raised her hand, "I thought that all homeroom assignments were final." Betsy was one of the best students in the school, but she was kind of a know-it-all. Avery sighed. She got so annoyed with Betsy always having the right answer.

"Betsy!" Maeve clapped her hands and shook her head. She couldn't help it; Betsy was really a nice girl and meant well . . . but sometimes she was just so clueless. Kevin was going to be in their classroom (too fabulous for words) and she wanted Betsy to chill out with the questions already. Thankfully, Ms. R came to the rescue.

"Betsy, no questions. Sometimes exceptions are made. Welcome to the class, Kevin. We're happy to have you." Ms. Rodriguez smiled and gestured Kevin to his seat.

Although the noise level went down, the activity level didn't: Anna and Joline, the Queens of Mean, began writing furiously in their notebooks. In a minute they were slyly exchanging folded-up slips of paper, and it didn't take a psychic to figure out what they were writing about! Katani shook her head. She was actually beginning to feel sorry for Kevin. He must feel weird to have all the girls whispering about him.

To Maeve, things were looking way up. She watched out of the corner of her eye, trying not to seem too interested, as Kevin strolled coolly down her row. When she turned her attention back to Ms. R, she could feel the back of her neck burning and hoped it wasn't turning bright red. She couldn't help it. Kevin Connors was completely adorable!

Chase Finley, one of Kevin's buddies, was sitting in the seat across from Maeve and gave Kevin a high five as he walked by. "Hey, dude, what's up? Ready to kick it up? It's up to us, bro. We're the only ones who have what it takes to win the Spirit Trophy," he whispered, but loud enough for everyone close to hear.

Maeve heard everything, and she couldn't help peeking over her shoulder to see Kevin's reaction. She was glad to see that he looked embarrassed. Chase could be a bit obnoxious on occasion.

Chase didn't seem to notice at all that Kevin looked uncomfortable. He glanced at the other boys in his area and pointed to Kevin. "This dude is the man." The others didn't seem to take offense and even seemed to agree, Maeve noted, because they all gave Kevin a high five or a "What's up, buddy?" as he went by.

Maeve took one last peek over her shoulder. As she did she felt her cheeks turn bright pink. She hoped the rest of the BSG didn't notice her reaction. Her friends, even Isabel, the latest BSG member, who had moved to Boston from Detroit, sometimes thought that Maeve's crushes went a little overboard. She had to kind of agree with them. Her seventh-grade crush list kept growing: first Nick Montoya, then Dillon Johnson, then Riley Lee, and now Kevin Connors. She just couldn't help herself.

Maeve had explained to the BSG exactly why she liked Kevin a few weeks before. "Look, I know Kevin is one of the popular athlete guys, but just because Anna and Joline like him doesn't mean he's a bad guy. He's dating Amanda Cruz. I think it was smart for him to pick a girl he can talk to about what matters most to him. And besides, it's just a crush. It's not like I'd steal him from Amanda or anything! I just think he's cute."

"And being good buddies with Chase Finley?" Katani had challenged her. "What does that say about him?"

Maeve had been stuck. "Well—maybe that he has a lot of patience?"

They had all laughed at that, even Maeve. The truth was, none of the BSG was crazy about Chase; he was kind of the guy version of Anna and Joline. He had their habit of taking little digs at other kids to try to make himself look good. So, none of them could really figure out why Chase was Kevin's best friend.

Ms. R went on with the morning routine, taking attendance and then starting off their first-period English class. Suddenly, Chase announced loudly, "Me and my man Kev are going to shake things up here at Abigail Adams. We own Spirit Week!"

Kevin looked even more embarrassed than he had when he first walked in. Katani whispered to Charlotte, "Why does Chase think it's okay to be so obnoxious? I just don't get it."

Charlotte shook her head and exchanged glances with Isabel, who rolled her eyes at Avery, who was bouncing up and down in her seat. Avery had way too much energy to sit still for long, and now she gave an extra bounce and shrugged her shoulders at Maeve.

Chase may be full of energy, but school spirit? No way, Maeve thought, twirling a curl around her finger. Then, as Ms. R began to ask questions about their latest assignment, Maeve tried to focus on her work. The only problem was that all she could think of was the upcoming dance. She just had to be on the dance committee. It was her destiny!

CHAPTER

3

"Don't Judge a Book
by Its Cover. . . ."

Third period was study hall, but Isabel had a permission slip to go to the art room instead. She was almost finished with her most ambitious project yet, and she was really excited about it! Her mother would be so proud—Mrs. Martinez hung her artwork all around the house. She said Isabel's cartoons were "inspirational."

The art room was empty, just as she'd hoped. Isabel stood still for a minute, observing the huge papier-mâché bird she had worked on for the past two weeks. Her caramel-colored eyes sparkled with pleasure. The bird was fashioned in jewel tones of green, scarlet, and yellow with a wingspan of almost three feet. Its head lifted proudly so the beak was its highest point. Isabel couldn't wait to put the finishing touches on it. She smiled to herself. If someone had asked her why she liked bird art, she wouldn't be able to put it into words. All she knew was that something inside her told her to go for it. So she followed her heart and created beautiful birds.

As she slipped into the paint-spattered smock, Isabel remembered her art teacher Mrs. Benigni's enthusiasm for the larger-than-life papier-mâché bird. "Oh, Isabel, this is really something special," she'd declared. "You know, I get art teacher specialty magazines, and one of them encourages us to send in our students' work when it deserves special recognition. When you're finished with this, if you'll give me permission, I'll photograph it and submit it. I want everyone to see the budding artist that you are!"

A photograph of her work printed in a magazine? That would be *incredible*. Her family would be blown away, except her sister, of course, who might be a little jealous of the attention.

She was circling the sculpture now, trying to decide whether to start with the wings, which were slightly lopsided, or the head, which needed to be tilted higher, when she noticed another sculpture off in the corner. It was obviously meant to be a fish slithering through the water and was made of some shiny, iridescent material. Isabel walked closer to get a better look. She rubbed her eyes. It was *bottle caps*, of all things!

What a totally crazy cool idea, Isabel thought. *Whoever did this is really talented.* She wanted to reach out and touch it but drew her hand back. Touching someone's artwork without permission wasn't respectful. It must have been one of the teachers who made the fish; it was just too creative and skillful to have been done by a student. But before she could find the artist's name on it, the door to the art room burst open and Maeve ran in, slightly out of breath.

"Iz!" she cried. "You are *just* the person I need!"

Isabel whirled around. "Hi, Maeve. What are you doing here?"

"Oh, I'm just stopping by. I have to get back to study hall to finish checking my music homework." Isabel admired Maeve's dedication to her schoolwork. She knew school wasn't easy for Maeve because of her dyslexia, and she and the other BSG were always there to support her and offer whatever help they could. Even though she struggled with school assignments, Maeve's talents in music, dance, and acting had to be seen to be believed. She was an outstanding performer, not to mention just full of plain old fun.

"What do you need?" Isabel asked Maeve.

"It's that committee thing—you know, for Spirit Week?" Isabel could tell that Maeve was about to launch into her usual speed talking. "I am definitely joining the dance committee, and you know what? I want to head it up. I know we can have the best school dance ever, even better than the stuff we usually do. So I just *have* to be the one running things. And *you* have to help me! If you sketch my ideas for the decorating and stuff, I can show them to the committee, and it'll be easier for them to see how fantastic it'll all be. I know they'll vote for me!" Maeve finished in a burst of excitement. Her blue eyes were shining brightly as she smiled at Isabel.

Isabel felt a pang of worry. "Oh, Maeve, I don't think I'll have time to sketch anything. I'm too busy finishing my art project right now. Just look at this thing." She gestured at the bird. "I need this finished in the next three days so my art teacher can photograph it and send it in to a magazine for consideration, and if it's not done by then, I'll lose my chance. It would be so cool to be in a magazine, and maybe someone would see my work and want to sponsor me for an art program next summer or something. Oh, I'm sorry, Maeve. I really wish I could help."

Maeve couldn't help looking completely crushed. She had gotten so excited about her plan for the dance committee that it hadn't even occurred to her that Isabel might not be able to help her.

Isabel felt terrible when she saw the expression on Maeve's face. Carefully, to keep the paint on her shirt from staining Maeve's pretty sweater, she leaned over and gave her a hug. "Well . . . maybe I can find a little time in between to help you out. Okay?"

She quickly added, "How about we work together on it for a half hour after school today. That should be enough time, right?" She just couldn't disappoint her sweet friend.

Maeve's smile burst forth. "I knew it, Isabel! I knew you wouldn't let me down!" She started to run out of the room before Isabel could say another word, but paused for just a second at the door. "Hey, love the bird!"

In a flash of bouncing red curls, she was gone.

Isabel let out a big sigh. She didn't *really* have time to help Maeve out with sketches for the dance committee. And knowing Maeve, when they sat down to work, she'd have a ton of enthusiasm, lots of great ideas, but would be struggling to figure out how to pull everything off. It would take Isabel forever to figure out what Maeve wanted and then do it. Maeve spent so much time gearing up for her Hollywood breakthrough, some of her ideas were bound to be over-the-top—interesting and exciting—but extremely ambitious. *What have I gotten myself into?* Isabel wondered. *Oh, well*, she thought. *I couldn't say no to her. Maeve is just like a beautiful, talkative parrot when she gets excited. How can you not love a parrot when it's chattering away, so happy and enthusiastic about everything?*

As she got out her art materials, Isabel thought more about birds and her friends. There were so many different types of birds in the world. Isabel was sure she could do a "What type of bird are you?" match-up with all her friends. The BSG had some things in common, but they each had unique personalities, just like different bird species. Katani with her tall, lean body and strong opinions would be a flamingo. Avery, because she never stopped moving, would be a blue jay, taking a million steps every minute. And Charlotte, who loved to write in her journal and study people, would be an owl, a wise bird that saw everything.

Before she knew what she was doing, Isabel had whipped out her sketchpad. Instead of working on the papier-mâché bird, she was consumed with new inspiration, drawing her friends in soft pencil as if they were birds. She whipped out a sketch of Maeve in just a few minutes. Bingo! There was the bright plumage of the parrot, the eager eye, the chattering beak. She was just about to add some dramatic touches to the bird's eyes when the door to the art room opened.

To Isabel's surprise, Kevin Connors walked in. She gave him a little wave and was completely stunned when he waved back and said, "Hey, Isabel. How's it going?"

How did Kevin Connors know *her* name? She knew Kevin because *everyone* knew him, but Isabel herself was fairly shy and was surprised that a hotshot like Kevin would know who she was.

Isabel dropped her pencil on the floor and watched it roll across the room. She flushed and bit her lip. *Now I know how Charlotte feels.* Charlotte was the BSG noted for her klutziness, and her friends were always gently teasing her for it.

"I'll get it." Kevin chased the pencil, snatched it up, and jogged over to where Isabel was working. "Here ya go."

"Thanks a lot." Isabel smiled shyly. "Are you here to work on a project?"

"Yeah," Kevin answered. "Hey, I've seen your work in here before. You're good. How long have you been . . . you know . . . into art?"

Isabel thought about it for a minute. "As long as I can remember, I guess," she admitted. "I've loved painting ever since I was a little kid, and now cartoons and papier-mâché are my favorites."

"Yeah, I've seen your cartoons in the *Sentinel*. I always look for them . . . they're really fun," Kevin complimented her.

"Thanks." Isabel relaxed a bit. Kevin Connors really was nice. She hadn't felt so comfortable talking to a boy since—well, she couldn't remember when!

"Hey, is that yours?" Kevin pointed to Isabel's papier-mâché bird.

Isabel felt a flush rising to her cheeks again. Unlike Maeve, too much attention made her nervous. "Yup," she said. "It's mine." Kevin didn't just give the bird a quick glance and move on to something else. He stood looking hard at it, his hands in his pockets, and then slowly circled it so he could see the bird from every angle.

Finally he shook his head. "This bird rocks! I can't get over your lines—they're so clean. The colors are perfectly balanced. You'd think that that scarlet red would crush the green, but you've used just enough so it doesn't. And how did you get the head to stay up like that?"

It was Isabel's turn to stare in astonishment. Kevin Connors, the school's star athlete, was talking like an art critic! She'd figured he was only interested in catching footballs or hitting baseballs, but art was obviously an interest of his. *I guess this is why they say, "Don't judge a book by its cover,"* Isabel thought.

"Hey," she said, "you talk like you're—"

"—really interested?" Kevin suggested. "Nah, I'm not interested. I just live for this stuff. That's why I had to switch homerooms. It was the only way I could fit another art class in my schedule." Isabel couldn't believe what she was hearing. A superstar athlete was secretly an artist in disguise.

Kevin shrugged and gave her kind of a silly grin. "Everyone around here just thinks I'm some jock who only cares about sports and nothing else. Don't get me wrong—I do like sports, but art is actually my favorite subject at school. I even think I want to go to art school when I graduate from Brookline High. You know, to study painting, drawing, and work in charcoal, maybe do a little sculpting—get a taste of everything so I can figure out what I really like and what I'm best at."

"You're kidding!" Isabel couldn't believe that there was anyone her age that was as passionate about art as she was. "That's what I want to do more than anything," she confided. "I think I already know what my favorite art thing is . . . cartooning. I love how you get to draw and think up funny sayings too."

"You should go for it, Isabel!" Kevin said encouragingly. "Seriously, your cartoons are awesome."

"You think so?" Isabel asked. Now she was flushing again, but she was also smiling. She couldn't believe that Kevin Connors—the boy everyone looked up to—was sitting there on the floor of the art room talking to her about art and listening to what she had to say. And he seemed to be really enjoying it!

"You know what?" Kevin said. "I think you're going to be a really great artist, Isabel. Honestly. Not just the cartoons but this bird—" He touched it lightly with one finger and shook his head in amazement. "Do you know how hard it is to get the balance and movement right in something like this? Well, I guess you must. But you did it. I mean, I know it's not finished, but the bird already looks like he could fly right out the door and down the hall to Mrs. Fields' office. And the crazy thing is that you're doing work like this *now*. Can you imagine what you'll be like when you're older and you've gone to art school?"

Wow, Isabel thought. *If I'm ever having a bad day, I'm going to go find Kevin Connors. He makes me feel like a superstar!* Isabel shifted the focus of the conversation off herself. "What about you?" she asked Kevin. "You must do some pretty cool projects too. Can I see something you've done?"

"Well, yeah." Now it was Kevin's turn to flush. "I'm trying to finish a project right now. That's why I came here during study hall. But the truth is, I can't seem to get it right, and half the time I want to just tear it up and throw the whole stupid thing in the trash."

"Which one is it?" Isabel looked at the projects scattered throughout the room. She wondered if Kevin had done the funny-looking robot in the corner. Even though it was kind of strange, it was pretty well-constructed, and Isabel thought it had a lot of potential.

But Kevin really surprised her. "Oh, it's the fish," he said, waving a hand at the corner and ducking his head as though afraid of her criticism.

"The fish?" Isabel turned to look again. The only fish in the room was the one made out of bottle caps; the one she was admiring before. "*You* did that?" she exclaimed.

Kevin grimaced. "Look, I know it really needs a lot of work. . . . I just . . ."

"Kevin, that fish is amazing!" Isabel cried. "I was looking at it a few minutes ago—I thought one of the teachers had done it! Look at how the bottle caps make it shimmer, as though the fish is gliding through the water and the light is turning it different colors. I can't believe you did that!"

"You think it's good?" Kevin looked amazed. "Really, Isabel? You think so?"

"Yes, definitely, it's so good!"

Kevin grinned at her a little sheepishly. "Wow. I was afraid when I turned it in they'd throw me out of the art department and tell me to stick to sports."

"No way!" Isabel shook her head emphatically. "That fish could win honors in any contest, Kevin, I'm completely serious. It's . . . it's . . . exquisite!"

"The same as your bird," Kevin insisted.

She grinned at him. "You know why I'm in a hurry to finish it? Mrs. Benigni told me she's going to send a photo of it to an art magazine, and she's hoping they'll print it."

"Hey, congrats! That would be awesome."

"Yeah, I'm really excited." She wanted to say more, but at that moment quick footsteps sounded in the hallway, and soon the door to the art room burst open.

This time it was Amanda Cruz, Kevin's girlfriend, and she looked furious. "I want to talk to you," she said sharply to Kevin, completely ignoring Isabel. Isabel noticed that Amanda was wearing a boy's gray hooded sweatshirt that looked totally out of place with her cute jean skirt and beaded jewelry.

Kevin didn't seem to pick up on the fact that Amanda was mad. "Okay," he said agreeably. "Amanda, you know Isabel Martinez, right? Um, she's in my . . . you know . . . Ms. R's homeroom."

"Hi," Isabel said with a smile.

"Hi," Amanda answered, but her tone was clearly dismissive. Even so, Kevin still didn't seem to get it.

"Amanda, check out the bird Isabel's making. Aren't the colors amazing?"

"Uh-huh," Amanda said, clearly not in the mood for art talk, or any talk that involved something other than Kevin and her. "Look, I don't have a lot of time," she said, turning her back on Isabel and speaking curtly to Kevin. "Come here a minute, will you?"

And without sparing Isabel another glance, she took Kevin's wrist and pulled him with her toward a corner of the room, which was filled with racks to hold wet paintings.

Isabel felt awkward and embarrassed by the whole situation. She wasn't sure whether Amanda expected her to leave or just to ignore them. But Isabel was here by special permission, and Amanda wasn't. So she turned her back on the couple and tried to get back into the bird sketches she'd been doing before Kevin first interrupted her.

Unfortunately, sketching was next to impossible, and though Isabel tried hard to concentrate, she couldn't help hearing bits of the conversation taking place in the corner. It became clear after just a few minutes that this wasn't just any boy-girl chat; Amanda and Kevin were *arguing*! *Oh my gosh!* How would they feel when they turned around and realized Isabel had heard almost everything they said? What was she supposed to do about it? *This is too weird*, she thought. The happy, comfortable feeling she'd had from talking with Kevin began to dissolve into embarrassment and tension, and her face started to flush all over again.

In the corner, Amanda was clearly angry and upset.

"Look," she was saying in a furious whisper, "I don't get what's going on here. I mean, I thought we were supposed to have lunch together, but whenever I try to come over and sit with you, you're in the middle of a big group of boys, which always includes Chase Finley. You know I can't stand him! Why can't we spend more time alone together?"

"I have lots of friends," Kevin protested. "I can't just ditch them. Besides, I like hanging out with my friends. And no one would care if you sat with us at lunch. I'm not trying to leave you out."

"Well, it feels like you are! We don't hang out at all anymore, Kevin. This isn't fun, and I don't think you even like me anymore. I don't even feel like I'm one of your friends, let alone your *girlfriend*!"

Isabel tried not to look up, but at that last sentence she couldn't help glancing at Kevin, who was flushing and avoiding Amanda's eyes. He stared at the floor and said, "Look, I still really like it when we play basketball together, and I think we should keep doing that, but . . . since this whole thing about us got around school, it's been weird, don't you think? I mean, wherever I go everyone wants to know why you're not with me. The first thing they ask when they see me is where you are. That's not what I thought was gonna happen when we first got started going out. . . . I thought it would just be fun."

"Well, what did you expect? I mean, everyone in this school knows who we are from sports. Didn't you realize they'd talk about us if we started going out?"

"I don't know." Kevin looked unhappy. "I never

thought about that. But now I feel like I have a new name; I should be called 'Dude, Where's Amanda?' Connors. It's not your fault, but it's really getting to me."

"Oh, thanks a lot, that is so nice of you not to blame me!" Amanda said sarcastically. "You think I wanted us to be talked about? You probably think I went around and bragged to people about us so they'd talk even more."

Isabel was trying so hard to not make it look like she was hearing what was being said that her fingers had tightened on her soft pencil. All of a sudden, it snapped in half, and the sound was like a firecracker going off in the art room.

Amanda whirled around, suddenly aware of Isabel's presence. "Do you mind? We could use a little privacy!"

Isabel looked at her, then at Kevin, who was beet-red and looking very uncomfortable. Special permission or not, it was definitely time for Isabel to make an exit—she couldn't stand any more of this!

Quickly, she gathered up her sketchpad and pencils and hurried out of the room, hoping she wouldn't drop anything until she got safely into the hall.

But just as she closed the door softly behind her and began to breathe a sigh of relief, her eyes widened. Lurking right outside the door, pretending to check out the posted artwork–but obviously spying—were Anna and Joline!

Great, just great, Isabel thought. The Queens of Mean were also the Queens of Gossip, and they would never keep their mouths shut. *How much did they hear?*

Most likely everything, because the first thing out of Anna's mouth was, "Oh, Isabel, I didn't know *you* were in there too. Tell me, is Kevin Connors *your* new art project?"

Isabel rolled her eyes. All Anna and Joline ever talked about was who was dating who, or anything that would make them look "cool." As Isabel walked away, she felt a twinge of anger and called back to the girls, "You don't even know what you're talking about. Why don't you just mind your own business?"

To her surprise, Anna and Joline actually backed off. Anna said, "C'mon, Isabel, chill. We're just kidding."

It didn't feel like kidding to Isabel. Her heart was pounding as she walked away from them without looking back. Being part of the A&J show was definitely *not* her idea of fun! But even so, it was better than being caught in the middle of the break-up scene in the art room.

The voices from the art room were getting louder as Anna and Joline turned back to listen. They heard the sound of a zipper and Amanda's voice saying plaintively, "Here, take back your precious hoodie. I don't think it's so special after all. And besides, it clashes with everything I own." Amanda sounded really mad.

Anna's eyes widened as she looked at Joline. "Whoa, did you hear that? She's giving back his *sweatshirt*. You know what *that* means."

Joline nodded her head. "Celebrity gossip! Amanda Cruz and Kevin Connors, *breaking up*?"

They slithered down the hall before the art room door opened again, and on both their faces was the satisfied look of a cat that had just swallowed a big bowl of cream.

4

Attitude with a Capital "J"

Charlotte had been thinking about Spirit Week all day. Now that she knew what it was, she was really excited. In fact, she wanted to use it as her feature article in the school newspaper, the *Sentinel*. She hoped Jennifer Robinson, the editor-in-chief, would approve her angle–that Spirit Week was a great tradition and the perfect way for students to make friends and promote the American spirit. Charlotte wondered what her friends Sophie from Paris and Shadya in Tanzania would think if she told them about Spirit Week. Shadya would probably laugh and clap her hands. Sophie would just shake her head in bewilderment. Charlotte thought how funny it was that everywhere she went people were so curious about Americans, like we were strange creatures doing strange things. Spirit Week would really make her global friends think that American students were a little off their rockers.

Charlotte knew better than to get her hopes up, though, when it came to her ideas for the *Sentinel*. Jennifer had tried to double-cross Charlotte on some articles in the past. It almost seemed as if Jennifer was jealous. Maeve, of course, was convinced that Jennifer was "positively green with envy" because Charlotte's writing was "superior." Thinking about Maeve's comment, she felt confident as she made her way to Ms. R's office. Charlotte had decided to run her idea by Ms. R instead of leaving it all up to Jennifer. Once burned, she wouldn't fall prey to Jennifer's tactics again. What was it her dad said . . . "Fool me once, shame on you; fool me twice, shame on me"?

"I think it's a great idea," Ms. R declared when Charlotte finished presenting it to her. "You've got a unique angle, Charlotte, and I hope Jennifer sees that. Let me know how it goes, okay?"

That was just what Charlotte wanted to hear. Now she had a teacher who knew her original idea, which should stop Jennifer from messing around with it or taking the credit! She hurried off to the newspaper office, only to find that Jennifer was already there, impatiently tapping her watch as Charlotte walked through the door.

"You're five minutes late," she accused Charlotte. "Now we've only got ten minutes before the next bell, and we've got a lot to cover. Please try to be on time in the future, will you?"

Charlotte blinked. Jennifer had been so nice at the beginning of the year and so enthusiastic over Charlotte's stories for the paper. Now, it seemed whatever Charlotte did was wrong. The BSG had all told Charlotte that Jennifer was "miffed" (that had been Katani's word) because everyone in school raved about Charlotte's articles, but it was still hard to take. It was no fun to be singled out and picked on, no matter the reason. Charlotte's stomach felt funny every time she had to interact with Jennifer.

She settled herself down in a chair and waited, but Jennifer didn't seem to actually be in any hurry to get the meeting started. She fiddled with her pencils and took her time sorting through her notebook.

As Jennifer stood up to officially start the meeting, Avery came flying in, closely followed by Chelsea Briggs, *The Sentinel*'s official photographer. "Hi, everybody!" Avery called as she and Chelsea took their seats. Avery never calmly walked into a room; she charged in at full speed.

Chelsea, who was much quieter than Avery, had settled down quickly, perhaps because she was still a little self-conscious about being overweight. Fortunately, though, during the seventh-grade class trip to Lake Rescue, Chelsea had become more confident and learned that she had a lot to offer, especially with her talents for photography and outdoor activities.

"All right, let's get started!" Jennifer directed the staff.

Charlotte noticed that Avery and Chelsea weren't scolded for being late, and they'd been later than she'd been! *Jennifer just doesn't like me*, Charlotte thought. *And nothing I do will ever change that.* Before making friends with the BSG, Charlotte would have been almost in tears over Jennifer's treatment of her. But Maeve, Isabel, Katani, and Avery were so supportive of her that Charlotte could now almost be indifferent to Jennifer's attitude.

Before Jennifer could say another word, Avery piped

up. "I've got a fantastic idea for the Spirit Week issue!" she announced. Avery wrote the "Move It!" column for the *Sentinel*, which talked about sports and other activities around school. "Listen," she went on, "there's going to be a coed tug-of-war and a huge basketball game. Do you know how much fun it's going to be to play a real, regulation game with boys and girls on the same teams?"

Even Jennifer couldn't resist Avery's excitement. "So what's your idea?" she asked, smiling.

"It involves Chelsea!" Avery announced, giving Chelsea a high five. "See, I think we should have Chelsea take lots of pictures of the students playing these sports, and I'll think of captions for all of them. You know there'll be lots of funny moments, and she always does a great job of snapping pictures at just the right time."

"That sounds fantastic!" Jennifer said warmly. Charlotte sat back in her chair. She was right—it was fantastic. But Jennifer never showed that kind of excitement about Charlotte's ideas. Suddenly a twinge of self-doubt struck her. Maybe her ideas weren't that great after all.

"Remember, though, Avery," Jennifer was saying, "we have to be careful that these pictures are just funny, and not mean. I don't want anyone to get their feelings hurt or be humiliated. Right?"

"Yeah, definitely," Avery agreed.

And Chelsea echoed, "I would *never* take pictures of stuff that would be *really* embarrassing." Charlotte knew that Chelsea was a sensitive person and that she would go out of her way to be sure her pictures didn't poke fun at anyone. After all, Chelsea knew what it felt like to be made fun of. Chelsea once told Charlotte that "fat kids always know that someone is making fun of them somewhere." Charlotte was relieved that Chelsea didn't have to face that anymore. After she showed off her wilderness skills at Lake Rescue, Chelsea gained the respect of the entire seventh-grade class . . . and a whole lot of confidence in herself.

"Fine," Jennifer said. "Then the 'Move It!' column is settled. Excellent idea, both of you. I can't wait to see those pictures—and captions!"

Charlotte just sat there, taking it all in. This afternoon, as soon as she got home, she would go visit her landlady, Miss Pierce, who lived on the floor below her. Miss Pierce always offered her tea, and even though she hardly ever left her house these days, she often had wonderful insights into people's behavior. Charlotte knew that if anyone could explain Jennifer's weird behavior, Miss Pierce could.

Jennifer called on every other staff member to talk about their assignments before she finally turned to Charlotte. "Let's make it quick," she said dismissively. "It's almost time to leave, so just tell me what you want to do for your next article."

Charlotte was stung. She was never long-winded. Jennifer was the one who could drone on and on and on at meetings, like she was the most important person in the world. But it was pointless to get mad about it. Carefully, Charlotte said, "Well, I've already talked to Ms. Rodriguez about this, and she thinks it's a fine idea." Jennifer sighed, as though what Charlotte was saying was just *too* boring.

Charlotte went on quickly, "I thought with Spirit Week happening, it would be a good idea to write about American spirit and give examples of it, like the rules about how to respect the flag and how people celebrate American spirit in so many different ways—like cheering for their favorite teams, or—" She faltered a little because Jennifer was rolling her eyes and the others didn't seem to think her idea was anything special.

Finally, Charlotte stopped talking altogether. She had thought her article would be terrific, but obviously nobody else did.

Jennifer waited until the room was completely silent before she asked, "And how many rules about the flag do you plan to list?"

"I don't know," Charlotte stammered. "I mean, I'm not completely sure of the details yet, I just came up with the idea this morning."

Jennifer ignored Charlotte's answer. "Well, what about the teams thing? How many teams and what kind do you plan to write about? College teams? High school teams? Local teams? National teams? Pro teams? Are you writing about the fans, or the teams themselves? Or have you not bothered to think about that?"

Jennifer was shooting questions at her so fast that Charlotte didn't have time to answer any of them, even if she'd had a clue what to say. Jennifer sounded as though she expected Charlotte to have finished all the research already, which was not the way these kickoff meetings usually worked.

She didn't do this to anybody else, Charlotte told herself.

Just me. She took a deep breath and tried to get her emotions under control. "Look, I'm just starting. But I think writing about all kinds of American spirit is exactly right for this issue, and for Spirit Week. Just let me take a shot at it. I won't let you down."

Jennifer shook her head, as though she couldn't believe how unprepared Charlotte was. "Well," she said finally, "I can't say you've done your homework on this, and I expect you to be more prepared before you write it. Just try to find something exciting to talk about, and don't resort back to your old travel stories, okay? I think you've used those way too many times already."

Charlotte was stunned. *How could Jennifer say something so mean?* To make matters worse, she'd actually been thinking about comparing American spirit to the spirit she'd witnessed in other countries. She thought that would be fun and informative, not boring in the least. Had she really talked about her own experiences so much that everyone else was sick of hearing it?

As if to confirm her fears, Avery jumped up and said, "Yeah, Char, this should be about Abigail Adams—we don't want to hear any more stuff about Africa or Paris." To make matters worse, Avery threw out her arms like a cheerleader and piped, "Abigail Adams . . . rah, rah, rah!"

Everyone else laughed, but Charlotte felt like her face was frozen. Was this really what Avery, one of her best friends, thought of her—boring Charlotte, who could only think of one thing to write about?

Suddenly Charlotte felt really upset, instead of just angry, at what was going on. Avery's making fun of her hurt a whole lot more than Jennifer's snide comments. Was this something a best friend would do? Charlotte didn't think so, and she didn't know how to handle it.

Fortunately, the bell rang, and everyone forgot about Avery's silly cheer in the scramble to get their stuff together. "Thanks, everybody!" Jennifer called. "Great meeting—and lots of great ideas, for the most part," she added.

Charlotte couldn't seem to get out of the room fast enough. Without a word to anyone, she rushed into the hall, intent on getting to her music class as quickly as she could.

Behind her, she heard Avery's voice. "Hey, Char, wait up!"

Charlotte didn't stop, and she didn't turn around. Instead, she kept walking, faster than ever. "Char, slow down," called Avery's voice from behind her. "C'mon!"

But Charlotte didn't slow down, and she was careful to keep her eyes forward as she hurried down the hall.

CHAPTER
5

Jazz It Up

When Charlotte arrived at music class, she headed straight for the center row, where the BSG usually sat. Maeve, Katani, and Isabel were already there, and all of them noticed that Charlotte looked upset.

"How was the *Sentinel* meeting?" Katani asked.

"Tell you later," Charlotte mumbled, unable to speak. Quickly she reached into her backpack for her music text and opened it to a random page. She just couldn't look at anyone, even her best friends.

A minute later, a frenetic Avery came tearing in and plopped down in the seat right next to Charlotte. "Hey, Char! Didn't you hear me after the meeting, calling you? Why'd you take off so fast?"

Charlotte couldn't think of a thing to say. She opened her mouth, but nothing came out. She didn't want to lie, but there was also no way she could tell Avery how much her comments had hurt. It wasn't just the comments either, it was that she had said them in front of Jennifer. Charlotte turned away. She could feel Katani's eyes on her, but she was afraid she might actually cry. That would be too humiliating.

Luckily, just then Ms. Ciara called the class to order. "Today we have a special presentation," she said, beaming. "In honor of Spirit Week, I'm going to share with you my very favorite music, because it's the music that gets *my* spirit going."

She waited for comments, but no one said anything. They were all waiting curiously. "It's *Birdland* music," Ms. Ciara announced dramatically.

"You mean 'The Chicken Dance'?" called out Chase Finley, and he smirked as some of the boys snickered and flapped their arms like chickens.

Ms. Ciara gave Chase a tolerant smile. "No. I mean great jazz music that began to appear around the end of World War II—can anyone give me that year?"

Betsy Fitzgerald's hand shot up immediately. Most likely, Betsy had memorized the dates of every big moment in history. She was always writing her reports ahead of time and doing elaborate research at the library, and she was a walking encyclopedia on almost any subject. On every test she took, Betsy would make up her own extra credit questions and answers to impress the teacher. *Poor Betsy, at least she's a nice girl,* thought Maeve as she looked over at Betsy's annoying, smug face.

Avery whispered to the BSG, "I bet Betsy already memorized all the Birdland songs, too . . . and wrote one of her own."

When Ms. Ciara called on her, Betsy declared, "World War II ended in 1945."

"That's right. And it was just around that time that Birdland music began to influence America. We're talking about great jazz players here—Charlie 'Bird' Parker, for whom Birdland was named; Count Basie, who had a great swing orchestra; and Thelonious Monk. These were gifted musicians who all had their own style, and each of them influenced Birdland in their own way. Look."

Ms. Ciara whisked down the blinds and turned off the lights. Then she pressed a button and started a slide show.

In fifteen minutes, Ms. Ciara covered all the highlights of Birdland music and the era in which it began. She showed photos of the major players, explained their specialties, and talked about the great music they'd created.

To everyone's surprise, it was actually pretty interesting. The slide show was exciting and alive, which was not always the case with school presentations. Dillon Johnson leaned over to Maeve and commented, "This sure beats that Beethoven guy." Maeve burst into giggles.

As Ms. Ciara flicked on the lights, she said, "Now I have an extra special surprise for you." She walked over to the door, peeked out, and gave a wave to someone in the hall. "Students, I'd like to introduce Michael Young and Sarah Finnegan from Brookline High's award-winning high school dance club. They're going to demonstrate the music of Birdland." Ms. Ciara held open the door and two older students entered.

The class turned to look at the dancers. Both of them looked like real professionals, dressed in 1940s-style dance outfits. Michael wore a pair of black trousers and a long-sleeved silk shirt. Sarah wore a bright red knee-length flared skirt, ankle-strapped high-heeled shoes, and a ruffled blouse. Maeve nearly fell out of her seat. She hoped that she could one day be on this dance team. The group was incredible, and Michael and Sarah were two of the best dancers on the team. She had to contain herself from rushing to the front of the room to join them.

"All right, class. Clear a space so our guests have enough room to dance," Ms. Ciara said.

The students jumped up and pushed their desks into a semicircle, creating a makeshift dance floor. Then Ms. Ciara moved to her stereo and spoke to the dancers. "Michael and Sarah, are you ready?" When they nodded, she pushed the button and the most amazing, toe-tapping music began to pour out. "This is Count Basie and his swing orchestra. Watch and listen." She presented the dancers with a dramatic swoosh of her hand. As bad as she felt, even Charlotte was a little excited.

After just a few bars, Michael and Sarah were dancing. No, not dancing—flying! They were spinning and swirling, first close to the ground and then stretching as high as they could. They danced close together, facing each other, and then far away, backs to each other, kicking and leaping and doing the most amazing moves.

Maeve sat entranced, her eyes wide. She was almost shaking. This was the most exciting dancing she'd ever seen . . . even better than hip hop, which was one of her favorites. Even the great Gene Kelly had never done anything this thrilling in any of his movies! Michael picked Sarah right up off the ground, and then she was spinning in his arms, her own arms extended to the ceiling, her head thrown back, legs high in the air. Michael dipped her, and Sarah's long blond hair was almost touching the ground. *Unbelievable!* Maeve thought. *I wonder what it feels like to be able to dance like that!*

Katani was hypnotized too, not by the dancers' moves, but by their clothes. *Those shoes are vintage, but totally back in style,* she thought. *They are too cool. . . . I need to find out where she got them! Are those PURPLE rhinestones sewn on the ankle straps? And who cut that blouse so Sarah could stretch in all different directions without pulling out the pleats?*

Riley had also been staring unblinkingly at the dance exhibition. Suddenly, he started to tap rhythmically on his desk. Then he jumped up. There was a drum set in the far corner of the room, and as the music pulsed cheerily, Riley began to lightly tap out the rhythms of the orchestra on the drums.

Maeve thought Riley's drumming made the whole thing even cooler, but she couldn't take her eyes off Michael and Sarah until the music finally ended and they stood together to take a bow. *That's it,* Maeve thought. *I just* have *to learn how to dance like that.* She looked around at the rest of the class. They were clapping enthusiastically for the dancers.

And then Maeve's blue eyes began to glow. *I've got it! The most fabulous idea for the Spirit Week dance!* A jillion little shivers ran up her back.

When the applause had ended, Ms. Ciara called, "Who'd like to come up and learn a few of the steps? Michael and Sarah would be glad to teach you."

A few students got to their feet, but the first one at the front of the room was Henry Yurt. In a broad exaggeration of an elegant gentleman, he bowed deeply to Ms. Ciara and held out his hand. "Madam, may I have the honor of this dance?"

Ms. Ciara, who usually shushed Henry, was definitely in the mood of Spirit Week. With a cool smile, she simply dropped into an old-fashioned curtsy, took Henry's hand, and faced him. Michael and Sarah showed them a few steps, and soon the goofy Yurtmeister was dancing with the tall, slender Ms. Ciara.

"Only the Yurtmeister could pull off something like this," whispered Maeve to Katani.

Henry caught on to the steps at once, but his face barely reached Ms. Ciara's shoulder. Watching him try to lead her was so funny that most kids in the class burst out laughing. It was good-natured laughter, though. Henry himself was grinning as he whirled Ms. Ciara around the floor. Chelsea Briggs couldn't help laughing too. She paused as the dancers got close to her, and then she snapped a photo of their happy expressions. She nodded at Avery. This was going to be a total A+ for the *Sentinel*.

Charlotte sat with her eyes turned toward the dancers, but she hardly saw them. She had shifted so her back was to Avery.

Avery kept staring at Charlotte trying to get her attention. Avery's usually lively dark eyes were quiet and bewildered. Finally, she got out her pen and scribbled a note, which she passed to Charlotte. *What's up—are you mad at me?*

Charlotte couldn't believe Avery even had to ask! *How can she not know what's bothering me? Can Avery be that clueless?* Charlotte fumed to herself.

She considered not answering at all. But then she thought, *This whole thing is getting weird, and talking about it might make things better.* Maybe Avery really didn't have a clue. So she turned over Avery's note and started writing.

Avery read the note and her cheeks turned pink. She wrote back, *I guess I blew it, huh? I'm really sorry. I just don't think sometimes.*

She started to hand the note to Charlotte, but her hand was unsteady as she held it out. To her horror, the slip of paper fell to the floor.

In a flash, Anna, Queen of Mean no. 1, had grabbed the note and tossed it to Joline, Queen of Mean no. 2, who started to read it out loud. Luckily, the music was still going, and most of the class was too focused on learning the dance steps to pay any attention. But Avery saw the stricken look on Charlotte's face. Charlotte clearly wished the floor would just swallow her up and take her far, far away. Being embarrassed in front of a whole class was one of Charlotte's worst nightmares.

Furious, Avery came to her friend's rescue. She tried to snatch the note from Joline. "That's not yours!" she snapped.

"Come on, Avery," Joline sneered. "I was just kidding. Since when did you get so sensitive?"

Avery opened her mouth to put Joline in her place—she had no problem standing up to the Queens of Mean—but just then she realized the room was too quiet. The music had stopped and Ms. Ciara was standing in their row, sternly looking at Avery and Joline. "I'll take that," she said crisply. When Joline silently handed her the note, the teacher glanced at it and then ripped it to shreds. "Girls, you know better than to pass notes in my class. Or in any class. It's disrespectful and only tells me that you weren't paying attention. Nothing you write in a note is so important that it can't wait until after the bell rings."

She walked to the front of the room and dropped the pieces of paper into her wastebasket. Charlotte, relieved, took a deep breath. *Thank goodness Ms. Ciara isn't one of those teachers who made students read notes out loud*, she thought. *That would have been completely humiliating*. She would have had to beg her father to pack up and move back to the Serengeti in Africa where no one could find her, especially the Queens of Mean.

What did Charlotte's father always say? "Never put anything down on paper that you wouldn't want made public." Now she knew just what he meant. It's easy to write something down, but it's not as easy to erase it if you change your mind.

Avery mouthed a genuine *I'm sorry* to Charlotte, and when Charlotte smiled at her, they both knew that whatever weirdness had been between them was gone. "I'm kind of glad Ms. Ciara caught Joline with that note," Avery whispered. "I bet Ms. C knew it wasn't really my fault. She's cool like that. Are you okay now?"

Charlotte gave her a thumbs-up. "I'm fine," she assured Avery. Charlotte was not one to hold a grudge.

Crossing the Line

The bell rang, and the class swept out into the hall, still raving about the dance demonstration. The girls were enthralled with Sarah's swishy skirt, her rhinestone ankle strap shoes, and those fantastic lifts, while Riley kept talking about the great rhythms of Count Basie's orchestra.

Dillon Johnson dismissed the dance talk as unimportant. "Hey, people, you're missing the whole point. The best thing about Spirit Week is these short classes. You hear me? S-h-o-r-t. As in, we have more time to do other things, more important things, like planning the sports events and doing stuff outdoors. Do you realize how much time we spend being cooped up inside at school day after day? We have to cram it all into this one week when we're actually *allowed* to have fun."

Dillon's cranky tirade was starting to get on his classmates' nerves. "Chill, Dillon," the always chill Nick Montoya advised him. "Spirit Week is great, but you gotta relax, man."

"Whatever, peeps. I'm just saying . . ."

"We got it, Dillon." Avery snickered, rolling her eyes. Avery was all for getting the most out of Spirit Week, but Dillon was being ridiculous. "You should have your own talk show or something," she suggested. "Ya know, talk show hosts are all about opinions, and you've obviously got a lot of those."

Dillon was smarting under everyone's snickers. "And *you* should be a dancer," Dillon retorted, and unexpectedly, he grabbed Avery and tried to throw her in the air, just like they'd all seen Michael do to Sarah. But Dillon wasn't as strong as Michael and Avery wasn't experienced at swing dancing, so she just tumbled down awkwardly into his waiting arms.

"Put me down!" Avery hissed at Dillon, her face turning red with embarrassment. "Put me down *now*, Dillon, I mean it!"

Dillon saw that Avery was really furious. Quickly, he lowered her to the floor. "Hey, Ave, come on, I was just kidding around. I didn't think you'd get all mad about it. It was just a joke, ya know, no big deal."

"I didn't think you had to be reminded not to pick people up and throw them around!" Avery fumed. "What do you think this is, the WWE?"

She yanked herself free from Dillon's arm and stormed off toward the cafeteria. *The short curse strikes again*, she grimaced. *If I wasn't so small and easy to toss around, Dillon wouldn't have even thought of throwing me in the air like that.* Avery wished some teacher had caught Dillon tossing her through the air like a football; they would've thrown him out of Spirit Week, and it would have been just what he deserved!

"Hey, Avery, wait!" Katani called to her.

"Did you see what Dillon just did?" Charlotte fumed as she hurried to catch up to Avery.

"Who could miss it?" Katani asked. "I bet Avery's ready to die of embarrassment."

Charlotte ran on to comfort Avery, while Katani caught up to Dillon, who was laughing uncomfortably at his own mistake and trying to get everyone else to laugh it off, too.

"Hey Dillon, you'd better grow up!" Katani advised him. "You totally embarassed Avery, and she's your *friend*. That was so not cool."

"Geesh, Katani, it was only a joke!" Dillon tried to defend himself. "If Avery had a sense of humor, she'd see that it was funny!"

"If she *didn't* have a sense of humor, you'd be in Mrs. Fields's office right now!" Katani shot back. "So just be glad she's a better friend than you are."

Maeve and Isabel were walking toward the cafeteria behind a crowd of other students. Maeve slowed down. Her idea for Spirit Week began to take on more color and dimension, and she just had to tell someone about it. Finally, she grabbed Isabel's arm to make her stop. "Isabel, I've just got to talk to you right now," she begged. "I have simply the most brilliant idea I've ever had for the Spirit Week dance theme."

"Oh yeah, I'm sure it's *brilliant*," came a shrill voice behind her, and Maeve realized that it was Anna, who was regarding her with one of her much-too-sweet smiles. Sarcastically, she added, "I'm sure it's the best idea *ever*."

Joline, who was just behind Anna, was snickering. Maeve looked at them both with sparks of anger in her eyes. But before she could say anything, Isabel snapped. She'd had just about enough of the Queens of Mean for one morning. Isabel stopped dead in her tracks and braced herself so that Anna crashed into her and Joline collided with Anna.

"Ouch!" Anna howled.

"Oh, Anna, I'm *so* sorry," Isabel said sweetly. "But

maybe you should pay a little more attention to where you're going."

Maeve grabbed Isabel. She wasn't sure how it happened, but things seemed to be rapidly spiraling out of control! The truth was, since early that morning, the day had been anything but normal, and Maeve was just getting tired of surprises.

"Listen, Iz, let's get out of here. I've got too much to tell you to waste any more time on annoying people."

The two girls started back down the hall, leaving Anna and Joline staring after them, but Maeve had already forgotten the incident. She had learned a long time ago that Anna and Joline were kind of like mosquitoes. Annoying, stinging, but certainly not life threatening. She immediately started chattering about how great her new idea was for the dance. Isabel just had to ask her, "Maeve, how can you let their comments just slide off your back like that? They make me so mad!"

Maeve shrugged. "You know, I think a few months ago I'd have cared a lot. But now it just seems like a waste of time. Anna and Joline aren't getting any nicer, so it's better to just stay out of their way when they get nasty."

"That's true," Isabel admitted. "I'll try to think of that next time they say something mean . . . which will probably be in about five minutes."

Maeve laughed. "You got that right. Okay, enough about them. Just wait until you hear my idea. This is going to be too fab for words."

6

The Buzz Begins

Maeve rummaged through the pockets of her school bag. "Oh, no!" she groaned. "I did it again! I mean this has just got to stop."

"What?" Isabel asked, bewildered.

"Forgot my lunch money again! It must be in my locker," Maeve said, blowing a curl out of her eyes. "It'll just take a second. Don't wait for me. I'll see you at the table." And she darted away toward her locker.

Isabel headed on to the cafeteria, but just as she reached the door, she spotted Kevin Connors. She wasn't quite sure how to greet him after the embarrassing break-up scene she witnessed that morning, but it hadn't been her fault she was there. She shouldn't feel awkward about it. It had nothing to do with her. Besides, Kevin had been so nice before all of the drama began.

So when Kevin got into the lunch line behind her, Isabel gave him a friendly smile.

He smiled back. "I can tell you're a real artist," he said.

Isabel looked at him questioningly. "You can? How?"

"Because, Isabel," Kevin said, "you have a big purple paint splotch on your shirt." He pointed to her sleeve. And as she looked down and discovered the enormous splotch, he started laughing.

When Isabel looked at Kevin, she saw that his eyes were smiling. He was laughing *with* her, not *at* her, and Isabel began to laugh too.

They laughed all the way down the lunch line, even though it wasn't really that funny. It was just one of those laugh fests that was contagious—once it got started it couldn't stop. Isabel and Maeve called those *laugh-a-thons*. It was on their list of totally favorite things.

The problem with this laugh-a-thon was that everyone in the cafeteria saw them. And so the buzz began. The buzz was definitely not one of Isabel's favorite things. The buzz could ruin your life. And now the buzz was spreading all over the cafeteria as if it were an infectious disease, and it was all about Kevin Connors and Isabel.

"Did you see that?" "Isabel Martinez and Kevin Connors!" "Well, I heard that he and Amanda are dunzo!" "And did you hear that they broke up in the art room—and Isabel was *right there*?" "No!" "I swear, it's true!" "Maybe she was the reason. . . ."

Leading the whisperer brigade, of course, were Anna and Joline. They were soon joined by Kiki Underwood, who was actually meaner, if that was even possible. The BSG called Kiki the "Empress of Mean" because she was so outright mean to anyone who was not in her exclusive group. The three chief gossipers were sitting at their usual lunch table, pretending to talk to each other but whispering loud enough for anyone who passed by to hear.

Amanda Cruz, who was waiting in line with some of her friends from the basketball team, saw the conversation between Kevin and Isabel and heard the buzz spreading around the cafeteria too. All morning she'd wondered whether Kevin was going out with someone else at the same time as he was dating her, and now it seemed that her suspicions were confirmed.

Amanda held her head high and pretended not to notice that anything unusual was happening. Her friends talked loudly and tried to ask lots of questions to distract her attention from what was going on. She carefully turned her back so she wouldn't see Kevin and pretended she was interested in the talk about Spirit Week, but she couldn't help sneaking glances around the cafeteria.

Isabel picked up a salad and some fruit juice and headed to the BSG table. Isabel wasn't exactly sure what was going on, but she could feel people looking at her when she walked by. So what! Two kids have a laugh-a-thon in the lunch line. *What's the big deal?* she wondered. *It happens every day.*

When she sat down, Maeve's comment took her slightly off guard. "Izzy, what's going on with you and Kevin?"

"What do you mean?" Isabel asked, trying to understand what Maeve was getting at. Had everyone heard about the whole break-up incident? Isabel slowly uncovered her salad and slit open the packet of dressing, waiting for Maeve to continue.

"I mean, the whole school is talking about it, like you are his new crush or something." Maeve gestured dramatically around the room. Isabel, looking around, realized with a sinking heart that Maeve was right. Dozens of eyes watched her furtively. Heads gestured from her to Kevin, who had sat down at Chase's table. Finally, Isabel's eyes rested on the Queens of Mean, who were looking directly at her with their piercing eyes. The pair looked like movie horror queens, ready to pounce on their next victim.

Suddenly, Isabel didn't feel hungry anymore. "Look," she murmured, "I was in the art room when Amanda stomped in looking for Kevin. Kevin and I had been talking about art stuff, and Amanda burst into the room, furious, and the two of them started fighting right in front of me. When I left the room, Anna and Joline were right there, and Anna made some comment about Kevin being one of my art projects. You know Anna, she'll spread any gossip she can, even if it isn't true."

"Well, what actually happened then? I mean . . . since you heard everything," Maeve probed.

Isabel looked uncomfortable. "I don't want to repeat it. It was supposed to be just between Amanda and Kevin."

"I can't believe those two," Katani fumed. "You and Kevin have every right to have a normal conversation. What did you guys talk about anyway?"

Isabel couldn't help flushing. "Well, the truth is . . . it was kind of nice to talk to him. He's really interested in art. You should see the fish he's making with bottle caps, it's . . . it's . . ." Isabel, searching for a word, threw her arms wide. "It's . . . incredible and sparkly . . . and it's so easy to talk to him about it."

"Kevin Connors is really into art *and he did something sparkly*? Now that's a surprise," Katani reflected.

"Well, it's true," Isabel confirmed. She was beginning to feel better and took some bites of her salad.

"So, what's the deal then?" Avery asked.

"Avery! Didn't you hear me? We're friends. *Just* friends. We had one little conversation about his project and my project."

"Yeah, but what about the laugh-a-thon? You two practically fell over just now in the lunch line," Avery sputtered in between bites of her sandwich.

"Can guys and girls be just friends?" Maeve wondered. "Doesn't romance always get in the way? I know for me it does. . . ."

"Of course they can!" Avery declared. "There's lots of things dudes and girls can do together and just have a good time, like going to a Red Sox game or bowling or ice skating or something."

"Like your friend Dillon picking you up in the hallway and embarrassing you in front of everybody?" Katani joked.

"That was wicked annoying," Avery admitted. "But *usually* Dillon and I do stuff like play sports together and hang out and talk at school or at Montoya's, and we are definitely *not* romantic." Avery stressed the last three words slowly and made a gagging noise to top it off.

"Well, I think you're right," Katani conceded. "Even when boys act like total fools, the truth is, you should be able to get along with them. And if you don't treat guys like real people, how can you ever decide whether you want to get closer to them and be their girlfriend? I think you have to start with whether you just like them or not as people. I think I'm against this swoony crush stuff. It just makes everyone crazy."

"Well, I don't think it's possible," Maeve announced. "Seems like that chemistry thing always gets in the way. A guy and a girl start *just talking*, and the next thing you know, they're going out, and it's bye-bye friendship. And if it doesn't happen, one of them gets a crush on the other and gets hurt if the other person doesn't like them back."

Isabel sighed. "Well, today I just feel like I'm trapped in some tacky soap opera. All we need are some glam costumes and cheesy music. I really don't like having everybody watch every move I make; it's like being in a huge fishbowl!"

"It's not that bad," Avery said. "So people are talking about you. You don't have to listen. Who cares what anyone else says, anyway?"

"Just try not to take it personally," Maeve advised. "Think of all the movie stars people talk about all the time– I read in *Stars Unlimited* the other day that a lot of movie stars try to ignore most of the rumors that start about them. Anyway, this'll blow over soon. I've got something else I want to talk to you about. I just *have* to tell you all about this idea I had in music class for Spirit Week."

"That reminds me!" Avery interrupted. "I've decided I want to head up the sports committee. I can't wait for the coed basketball game—we're gonna show those guys that girls rule! It's about time girls and boys play together on a team. Don't you think picking the teams will be the best?"

Maeve sighed. *There goes one vote for the dance committee.* The sports committee met at the same time as the dance committee, and no matter how fast Avery was, she couldn't be in two places at the same time.

Maeve opened her mouth again to start explaining to the BSG her big idea about the dance, but suddenly Charlotte broke into the conversation, telling them all about Jennifer's miserable attitude toward her Spirit Week article. "She hates me. And she hates my writing. You should have heard the nice things she was saying to everyone else on the staff except me! You heard her, Ave! She told me in front of everybody to stop writing about my travel experiences— that I'd done too much about them already. It would have been one thing to talk to me about that privately, but she embarrassed me in front of the whole group!"

"Look, Charlotte," Katani advised, "I told you before that Jennifer's just plain jealous, and that's what all this is about. You've just got to let this one go, girl. Jennifer's like your boss, and you don't want to quit your job, so you'll just have to live with it."

"But what could she be jealous of?" Charlotte protested. "It's not like my stuff is going to win the Pulitzer Prize or anything. I mean, it's not better than hers, anyway."

"Now wait just a minute, Charlotte Ramsey," protested Maeve. "Jennifer's stuff is *so* not better than yours and she's a whole year older." Maeve looked around the table at the BSG and held up her soda. "I say we toast Ms. Charlotte Ramsey as the best writer we know."

A chorus of cheers met that statement, and finally Charlotte looked at her friends gratefully. "You guys are the best," she said. "Seriously, what would I do without you?"

Maeve sighed again. She couldn't interrupt now, not when Charlotte was enjoying a moment of support.

While the BSG finished their lunches, Charlotte explained her current dilemma. "But maybe Jennifer's sort of right. Instead of writing comparisons or trying to use stuff outside of Abigail Adams . . ." She gave a smile to Avery, "I think I should just write about what spirit is *here*, at our school and in our town. That's what Spirit Week is about, right? I'll interview students about their views and write them up for the article. Maybe I can interview some adults too, like Mrs. Fields and Yuri and Mrs. Weiss and Ms. Pink." She looked around at her best friends. "And I think I'll start with you and what *you* think spirit is." She looked expectantly at the BSG.

There was silence at the table for a minute. No one knew what to say. Then Isabel volunteered, "What about art? I think art gives me spirit. It makes people feel good and shows that ordinary things can be really beautiful when you see them from a fresh perspective."

Avery started doodling in her notebook, and when she ripped out the sheet and showed it to them, they all burst out laughing, even Isabel. Avery had drawn some sort of person leading a cheer, but it was terrible, like something a four year old would draw.

Avery pretended to be outraged that everyone was

laughing at her drawing. "What's wrong with it? I think it's good. I think it shows *my* spirit."

At that goofy remark, Charlotte, who had taken out her notebook, dropped it and her pencil on the table and put her head in her hands. Her shoulders were shaking with laughter.

All the BSG were being so loud that other tables started to look over at them. "Hey, what's going on over there?" called Chase with his usual "I'm so cool" confidence. "You girls having a fight or something? Now that doesn't sound like it's in the spirit of Spirit Week." Chase shook his finger at them condescendingly.

"BSG fight!" chanted a group of girls at another table.

"We are not fighting!" Charlotte called back.

Avery added, "We're just having a good time at lunch, Chase. Are you jealous?"

Katani and Isabel were still laughing, more softly this time, when Chelsea Briggs popped up behind them and snapped a photo. "Oh, no!" Katani gasped. "You caught me with my mouth open."

"You were showing *your* spirit," Maeve giggled.

"I was showing my *molars*," Katani moaned. "And I bet that picture pops up twenty years from now when I'm a business executive and just ruins my reputation."

That helped them all calm down. Charlotte noticed the cafeteria starting to empty out and looked at the wall clock. "Hey, we only have five minutes before class. We'd better get packed up quick!" The girls jumped up and cleared the table, wiping it off after they stacked their trays so it would be clean for the next students.

As they were finishing, Maeve remembered that she still hadn't had the chance to tell her friends her fabulous idea. "Hey, guys," she started, but just then, Chase Finley came by, smirking at Isabel.

"So what's all the noise about, Isabel? You telling 'em all about Amanda and Kevin breaking up today? I heard you know all about that."

Isabel stared at him. She couldn't believe he'd make a joke like that! She was so appalled that she couldn't even think of an answer, which made Chase think he'd really gotten her. He cackled in her direction as he walked away.

"That boy needs some social IQ lessons!" Katani fumed. "He always acts like his mouth hasn't heard from his brain in a month!"

"Come on, guys, we better go," Charlotte warned. "We're all going to be late if we don't hurry!"

As they were rushing out the door, Avery saw Dillon waiting for her just outside, his eyes hopeful. "Uh, Avery, can I talk to you a second?"

The others looked at her, but she just shrugged. "You guys go on. I'll see ya later." She turned to Dillon, whose face was reddening. "Well, this better be quick, because that's all I've got—about one second. What's up?" She didn't think she had to be too friendly to Dillon after the way he'd treated her in the hall.

But Dillon seemed genuinely miserable. "Ave . . . I just wanted to say I'm really sorry for what I did. You know, throwing you in the air before. It was a–a totally dumb thing to do, and I, I don't even know why I did it. It seemed like a funny joke at first but I guess it was really stupid.

Anyway, I'm really sorry. I mean, I like being friends with you and stuff, and I don't want you to feel bad."

It wasn't the smoothest apology in the world, but it was sincere. Avery looked suspiciously at Dillon, but he looked uncomfortable and unhappy. Obviously he had been thinking about what he did and realized it was wrong. And it took a lot of courage to come apologize. "Well," Avery said grudgingly, "I guess it's okay. But don't ever do it again, all right?"

"I won't!" Dillon said quickly. "I promise. Hey, you going down the science hall?" Avery nodded. "I am too. Let's go."

They had to hurry, because there were only about thirty seconds left to get to class, but Dillon talked Avery's ear off all the way to her classroom. "You know," he said, "you should think about going out for the sports committee. I bet you could even head it up. Everybody knows you're great at sports, and I'm sure they'd vote for you."

"You think so?" Avery asked. She wasn't going to tell Dillon she was already planning to go all out for the sports committee!

"Oh, yeah!" Dillon assured her. "I'd vote for you. That's one vote right there!"

"Well, I might think about it," Avery said as she opened the door. "Bye, Dillon." She held out her hand for a high five and Dillon grinned as he slapped her hand with a *thwack*.

7

Movie House Magic

aeve managed to get all the way home after school without having had a single chance to tell her friends about her glorious idea for Spirit Week. She was so frustrated because it was such a great idea, and she just had to tell *somebody*!

That's it, she thought. *I'll IM everyone tonight and call an emergency BSG meeting at Montoya's for tomorrow morning.* Besides getting feedback for her idea, she could start her day with a frozen hot chocolate—that would almost make up for the crazy morning she'd had that day!

Sam was already home when she walked in. Before she could even drop her backpack, he demanded, "Hey, wanna play cards with me?"

"Where's Mom?" Maeve asked, ignoring his plea. She was not in the mood for cards, especially since her brainiac little brother almost always won!

"She went to the grocery store. She said we needed

chicken for dinner. C'mon, will you *please* play cards with me? I'll let you beat me at Spit."

"Sam!"

"Half an hour. Twenty minutes," Sam bargained. "Okay, *ten* minutes. C'mon, Maeve!"

"Sorry, Sam. No time. I've got an amazing idea. This is going to be absolutely the *best* week of my entire life!"

Sam looked at her. "Bet I can guess why."

"Oh really?" Maeve looked back at him, her hands on her hips.

"I know I can." Sam smirked. "Bet our allowances this week that I can."

Maeve knew better than to trust Sam when he bet their allowances on anything; she'd lost hers to him many times before. But there was no way he could know why this week was going to be the best ever. Sometimes you just had to pay out to get want you wanted.

She grabbed Sam's hand and shook it. "Okay, boy genius, you're on."

"Hmm, let me think about it. This is hard." Sam pretended to search the ceiling for an answer. He scratched his head and furrowed his brow. Then he looked up. "I got it. You're starring in the new school play, *Bride of Dracula*."

Maeve gave him a dirty look and flung a stretchy headband in his direction.

"Okay, okay. I get another guess." Sam thought for a minute. "I know. You're gonna be lead singer for Riley's new band, Mole and the Caterpillars."

"*Sam!*"

"No, I know! The whole seventh grade except you got

really bad food poisoning, so you're the new head of the math team!"

Maeve swung around, her eyes blazing.

"I'm kidding!" Sam yelled. "Can't you take a joke?"

"That's not funny, and you know it!" Maeve was trying not to let her eyes well up. She was pretty easygoing about jokes, but not when it came to math. It felt awful to be teased about her worst subject, especially by her genius little brother.

She shook it off and put out her hand. "Game over, you've had your guesses. You're not even close. I'll take *your* allowance now, thank you very much!"

"One more guess!" Sam cried. "Just one more."

"You've already had three. That's way more than you should have gotten. Give me your allowance. Now!"

"One more! I know I can get it," Sam insisted. "What if I act it out?" In a minute Sam was cartwheeling all over the living room, chanting, "Rah, rah, rah, sis, boom, bah, gooooo, Abigail Adams!" Sam finished off with a flying split in the air.

"Sam, that's so not fair!" Maeve complained. "Who told you about Spirit Week?"

Sam laughed triumphantly. "I'll take your allowance NOW, Maeve."

"Who told you?" Maeve demanded. "You knew somehow, I know you did; you couldn't have just guessed!" And she promptly started to chase Sam around the kitchen table. Sam gave his ear-piercing warrior cry and began to run for his life, but Maeve could be quick on her feet and within seconds she was at his heels.

Maeve had her fingers stretched out to grab Sam when she heard her mother shout, "What are you two *doing*?" Ms. Kaplan came in with a bag of groceries. "I'm gone for two minutes and I can't trust you to behave? What's going on here?"

"We're just settling a little disagreement," Maeve explained carefully. She knew it was best to say as little as possible.

"It's Maeve's fault!" Sam cried. "She lost a bet with me and she doesn't want to pay up. She owes me her whole allowance!"

"You two know better than to bet!" Maeve's mother dumped the grocery bag on the kitchen table and turned to face them, arms folded. "Now, tell me the whole story!"

Maeve groaned. Sometimes it seemed like her mom made things way more complicated than they needed to be. It took a few minutes for Maeve and Sam to tell both sides of the story. When they'd finished explaining, Ms. Kaplan said sternly, "You both deserve to lose your allowances. I've said it before: no betting allowed in this household. Sam, I expect you to apologize to Maeve for those remarks about the math team. And Maeve, next time you're trying to 'settle a disagreement,' find a better way to do it than chasing your brother around the house."

"Sorry, Maeve," Sam muttered.

Maeve didn't think he was especially sorry at all, unless he was sorry to have gotten caught! If her mother had come in five minutes later, his attitude would have been totally different.

"At least," Maeve said to her brother, "tell me how you

found out about Spirit Week. I didn't think anyone outside Abigail Adams knew."

"Harry told me," Sam answered. He went to the kitchen to get plates and silverware to set the table.

"Harry?" Maeve didn't remember a friend of Sam's with that name. "Harry who?"

"Harry Wooster."

Now she was really puzzled. "Who's Harry Wooster?"

"What're you, the FBI? Harry's my new friend." Sam took down three plates, three bowls for salad, and grabbed a fistful of knives and forks from the silverware drawer.

"Okay," Maeve said, trying to be patient. "And how does *Harry* know about Spirit Week?"

"His cousin told him," Sam said, plopping the plates and silverware on the table. Maeve carefully took three glasses from the cupboard and filled them with milk.

"And . . . ?" she asked. "Who's his cousin?" Sam gave her an exasperated look, which she returned. "Look, just spill it, Sam! This is getting ridiculous!"

Sam smirked, but when he saw the total lack of patience on Maeve's face, he knew it was time to stop teasing her. "Okay, okay. Harry's cousin goes to Abigail Adams. She wants to be head of the dance committee or something, and she was talking about it when we saw her after school. That's how I knew."

"And her last name is Wooster?" Maeve couldn't think of any Abigail Adams student she knew with that name.

"No, that's *Harry's* last name, dopey. His cousin's name is Betsy Fitzgerald."

Maeve groaned. "No! Not Betsy Fitzgerald! She wants

to head the dance committee? Why me? I'll *never* stand a chance against her!"

If the school ever voted on "The Student Most Fanatic About Building an Impressive Résumé," Betsy Fitzgerald would win in a heartbeat. She was the most hyper-organized person Maeve had ever met, even more than Katani. Even if Betsy didn't have a great original idea for a dance theme, it wouldn't matter. She would campaign like crazy, work overtime, make charts, rally the students, and do whatever it took to be voted the head of the dance committee. Maeve knew kids would eventually give in and vote for Betsy. She'd convince them that she'd do a good job . . . and she probably would.

I stand NO chance at all of getting this, a disappointed Maeve told herself. *And my great idea is going to rot before anyone even finds out about it!*

As she thought more about the Birdland theme, she got upset and realized that she couldn't just give up. She just had to stick up for herself and go for it, even if the most together person in the whole of Abigail Adams wanted to be in charge. Maeve knew she had the best possible idea for a dance theme and that it deserved to be heard by everyone. She wasn't going to give up and creep away without even trying just because Betsy Fitzgerald also wanted the job. Besides, Betsy probably wanted everyone to dress up as Harvard students!

I need a plan. Maeve made a mental note. *And I need some advice. Who can I go to who'll help me?*

Then she realized: Who did she always run to when she needed help, especially when she had a fabulous idea?

"Mom!" she shouted, running into her mother's bedroom where her mom was changing into some sneakers. "Mom, can I run down to the Movie House right now? Please? It's an emergency."

Her mother looked at her strangely. "Do you have to go right away?"

"It's totally critical. I really *need* to see Dad."

Her mother nodded. "Well, for a little while. Don't take too much of his time while he's working."

"I won't," Maeve promised. She turned and bolted down to the Movie House at a run. It used to be the family business, but that was before her parents had separated and her mother got an office job. Before the separation, Ms. Kaplan and Mr. Taylor had run it together. Maeve loved sitting in the soft, comfortable plush velvet seats, watching old movies, eating real movie popcorn, and dreaming about the day when she would be up there in lights.

It was strange sometimes to think that her parents weren't together. At first it bothered her a lot. She would cry into her pillow at night and ask her parents "but why?" But her parents could never really answer why in a way that made sense to Maeve. The only good thing was that they both stayed in Brookline and that made it much easier to tolerate the separation. Still, though, some days she wished it could go back to the way it was when they were all together.

Right now, though, she needed to concentrate on the immediate . . . her idea for the dance. She found her dad, as usual, in the projection room, his thick dark hair slightly rumpled. "Hi, honey," he said with surprise, giving Maeve a big hug. "What's up? Isn't it dinnertime?"

"I know, Dad, but I really just had to see you."

"Well, I'm glad you're here. You've got to see this new foreign short film that came in today—it's really moving. It's about Iraqi war orphans starting a business to sell sweets to American soldiers."

When her dad got excited about a movie, Maeve knew better than to argue. She sat with her head on her dad's shoulder while he screened the movie just for her.

The movie told the story of Abdullah and his sister Maji, whose parents had died, but the siblings refused to go to the local orphanage where other parentless children lived. Instead, the two snuck into the local bakery every night and used the bakery equipment and ingredients to make cookies, which they then sold to American soldiers. The soldiers loved the cookies and the money kept Abdullah and Maji alive.

When it was over, Maeve wiped a few tears from her eyes. She saw her dad doing the same; he was a nut for movies just like she was. "It was great, Dad," she said. "But I don't know if I could be strong like that if something happened to you."

"Well, I wouldn't worry too much about it," Mr. Taylor told her. "The world of international film wouldn't be able to function without me."

"Dad!"

"Plus I'm strong and healthy *and* a black belt in Tae Kwon Do." Her dad jumped up and proceeded to kick and chop his hands in the air. It looked like nothing Maeve had ever seen before—it might be the Three Stooges' version of martial arts, but it wasn't anything Jackie Chan had ever done!

Maeve started to giggle, which turned into laughter, which caused tears to stream down her face. Her dad joined in, and they laughed until their stomachs hurt.

When they finally settled down, Maeve explained Spirit Week to her dad and told him how badly she wanted to head the dance committee. Even though she knew Betsy Fitzgerald was in the running, her idea was too exciting to give up. "I've got an absolutely amazing theme, Dad," she said, "and I know nobody else could have a better one."

"Well that's confidence for you. What is it?"

"The dance theme will be . . . Birdland," Maeve announced dramatically, her eyes glowing with her vision of it. "We learned all about it in music today, and I think it's the coolest music I've ever heard! And Ms. Ciara brought in two high school students from the dance club to show us the dances that went with it—Dad, the dancing is fabulous! It made me want to quit hip hop and start jazz dance lessons right away. Not really, but you know what I mean. I know everyone's going to love this, and it'll be the most original dance we've ever had—don't you think so?"

"Hey, honey, you're preaching to the choir here."

Maeve was confused. "What does that mean?"

"It means I'm not going to argue with you about it. I love jazz music, and I love the old Birdland stuff. So any dance that has that for a theme sounds perfect to me. Now, let me think. . . . What did I do with them?"

Maeve knew better than to interrupt her father when

he was thinking through an idea. He walked along the walls of the projection room, where there were big bins that held old movie posters. "Ah, yes, I think they're in here."

He rummaged for a few minutes and finally pulled out two movie posters. "Here we go. These movies were made right at the time Birdland was going strong, and this one even has a scene set in the Cotton Club in Harlem. Same bands, same music . . . look!"

Maeve looked closely and was soon mesmerized by the women dressed in the slinky, elegant clothes she'd dreamed of for the dance. The men wore strange-looking suits—"zoot suits" her dad called them—with pants that ballooned from a tight waist to big puffy legs and then snugged in again at the ankles. Even though it was kind of a weird style, Maeve thought the dancers looked fantastic.

Her father gave her a bunch of posters to take to school. "And tell you what," he added. "Give me a day and I'll put together some film clips for you, showing some great scenes from that era. I'll bet when the committee sees it, they'll flip out."

"I know they will!" Maeve cried. "Oh, Dad, thank you! I knew you'd have some great ideas for me!"

She had to leave then, so her father could finish his work for the evening, but Maeve was more passionate now than she had been when she first brainstormed her great idea. She could absolutely see the dance in her mind—everyone in fantastic clothes doing those great spins and lifts Michael and Sarah had demonstrated for them today, twirling across the decorated gym. Maybe she could even talk Riley into dressing his band in zoot suits, so they could match the theme.

It's going to be positively perfect, Maeve promised herself. *The very best dance Abigail Adams has ever seen!*

8

Dinner Dish

Getting dinner ready with her sister Kelley was not on top of Katani's list of favorite things to do. Katani adored Kelley, but Kelley's autism often put a strain on things. Katani was methodical by nature, and it was frustrating to have all of Kelley's disruptions. They had to do everything in very small steps, so Kelley could help without getting confused or upset. Even having their grandmother, the school principal, in the kitchen with them didn't make things run as smoothly as Katani would have wanted.

I shouldn't be like this, Katani told herself. *Kelley's such a sweet sister and I wouldn't want her to realize that she makes me crazy sometimes. But I just can't help it.* Suddenly, she remembered what her mother had told her a long time ago. She had ruffled Katani's hair and said, "Honey, I know it's not easy to have a sister like Kelley. It requires so much patience. But Kelley can't help herself, and when you grow up you will thank Kelley." When Katani had asked why, her mother answered, "Because by dealing with Kelley, you will have learned how to be tolerant when people make mistakes. And you will be a better person for that." Katani took a few deep breaths and felt a bit better, but it was hard. Kelley was really over the top today.

Somebody at school had told Kelley about Spirit Week that afternoon, and ever since, Kelley had been talking about it a mile a minute and asking a million questions. Katani tried to answer when she could, but she didn't know answers to all of the questions. When Kelley didn't get an answer that she was satisfied with, she made up something funny and laughed at her own jokes.

Mrs. Fields checked the oven, where they'd finally — after several false starts and unfortunate spills — popped in a shepherd's pie in a crust with chopped meat, mashed potatoes, and spices. "It smells delicious," she told her granddaughters. "Now we'll let it bake for about an hour, and we'll make a salad."

"Carrots are health food," Kelley sang out loudly. "Carrots make you healthy. Health comes from carrots. Carrots are healthy. Carrots are good for you. . . ."

Katani tried to smile, but she knew that once Kelley got a song into her head, she'd sing it again and again, until it was unbearable. And then Katani would find herself singing the same song in the shower the next morning, unable to shake the tune from her memory. Mrs. Fields put a gentle hand on Kelley's head to stop her singing and swiftly changed the subject. "What committee are you interested in working on for Spirit Week?"

"I've got my own committee!" Kelley interrupted.

"Mr. Bear and I are going to be on the same committee." Mr. Bear was her favorite stuffed animal. She often carried him around to "hear" what everyone else was doing. Whenever Kelley misplaced Mr. Bear, which happened on occasion, she would be inconsolable until the loved and tattered bear was found.

"What committee are you going to join, Kelley?" Mrs. Fields asked.

"The marching band committee!" Kelley announced. "Mr. Bear and I are going to be on the marching band committee. Miguel's marching band is rad, totally rad." She went on repeating, "Rad, totally rad" again and again.

Kelley was always talking about her friends at school. Katani was so glad that there was a good program at Abigail Adams for kids who needed some extra help.

"I don't think they have a marching band committee, Kelley," said her grandmother. "I'm sorry, sweetheart."

"They do!" Kelley insisted. "I saw them today. Mr. Lewis was the head of it, and he was marching up and down, just like I will. I'm going to practice right now." And soon she was marching up and down the hallway outside the kitchen, her arms stiff, her legs pumping rhythmically.

"Don't you want to practice with Mr. Bear?" Katani suggested gently.

"Oh, yes! Yes! I do, do, do! Thanks, Katani." Kelley ran off to her room to get Mr. Bear and march with him up and down the hallway, stiffly, like she imagined a soldier would. "Forward, march!" Kelley repeated over and over as she continued the march.

"Maybe you can organize an animal parade." Mrs. Fields smiled, watching Kelley.

"When we march," Kelley said breathlessly, "we have spirit too, just like everyone else!"

Katani cheered up as she watched her sister march. "Grandma, who's Kelley's friend Miguel?" she asked.

"Oh, he's a very nice boy," Mrs. Fields answered. "I'm sure you'll meet him one of these days."

Isabel tiptoed out of her mother's room and closed the door softly behind her. She didn't like to wake her mom when she was resting comfortably. Having multiple sclerosis had sapped her mother's energy badly these last few months. Her new doctors in the city were helping to keep her MS in control, but Mrs. Martinez still spent a lot of her time resting. Isabel had so wanted to tell her mom all about Spirit Week and the curious conversation she had with Kevin today, but it would have to wait. Isabel left a cartoon of a little bird on the nightstand next to her mother's bed. Her mother loved her birds. She said it made her feel "cheery inside," so Isabel was always creating new cartoons, paintings, and sketches to cheer her up. At least when her mom woke up, she'd know Isabel had been thinking of her.

Without having her mother to talk to, Isabel felt restless. Following the scrumptious smells that were wafting out, she wandered into the kitchen. Her older sister, Elena Maria, was making her famous burritos for dinner. They were Isabel's favorites. Elena Maria did a lot of the cooking for the family, since their Aunt Lourdes worked as a nurse and their mother was often too weak to do many household chores. Besides, Elena loved to cook, and she was always trying out new recipes. She and Isabel had talked about opening their own restaurant someday, a family-style place with the best food, and beautiful artwork hanging everywhere. Elena said there weren't very many good Mexican restaurants in Boston, so she was pretty sure Casa Elena's El Pompeo would be a hit.

"Mmm, smells so good," Isabel complimented Elena's cooking as she took a small bottle of apple juice from the refrigerator. She was already hungry, but she wasn't about to spoil her appetite. Elena's burritos were worth waiting for! "Are we eating early tonight, Elena? I can't wait much longer!" Isabel wanted to chomp into the best burrito this side of Tennessee immediately.

"In a few minutes." Elena rolled up another flour tortilla filled with meat, beans and cheese and slid it onto a tray in the oven. "I'm not sure yet, but I think I may be going out later with Jimmy . . . to study . . . at the library."

Isabel rolled her eyes. "Most girls would *know* whether or not they were going out," she told her sister. Isabel wasn't crazy about Elena's high school boyfriend. She thought her sister should be treated much better than she was. Jimmy always made plans with Elena and then broke them at the last minute, and Elena pretended not to be upset. Isabel thought that high school relationships seemed way too complicated.

"Stop it, Isabel." Elena had heard this before. "Jimmy's so busy. He's a real serious athlete. And you know when he starts thinking about football, he gets distracted and can't handle anything else."

Isabel couldn't stop herself from making another comment. She hated seeing her sister treated disrespectfully by her own boyfriend, and she really wanted to get through to her. "You mean the things everyone should remember, like showing up on time and calling you just to talk and letting you know that he cares about you? Things like that?"

"I said stop it!" Elena didn't like hearing criticism, especially of her boyfriend. "He's cute and funny and maybe he thinks a little too much about football. That's it. But he's my boyfriend, so it'd be nice if you could at least *try* to like him."

Isabel took a sip of her juice. She didn't want Elena to feel bad, so she tried to speak more gently. "Sorry, Elena. I just want you to be happy." She tried a different approach. "He thinks so much about football, but you couldn't care less about sports. Is that really a great match, Elena? Do you have anything in common with him?"

"You're too young to understand," Elena said dismissively. "Here." Elena took the lid off the pot of soup she was stirring and pulled a big spoon out of the drawer. "Taste this and tell me what you think."

Isabel knew Elena was trying to change the subject, but she wanted a taste of the soup. As she slurped, Isabel thought that since Elena loved cooking so much, she should hang out with Avery's older brother, Scott. Avery and Isabel had schemed about getting them together, but because of Jimmy, they hadn't done anything about it. *One of these days*, Isabel told herself as she tasted the tortilla soup. "Perfect," she decided. "I can't wait for dinner." She gave her sister a little smile to smooth things over.

"Mom awake?" Elena Maria asked.

"No. And I really wanted to talk to her today."

"Why's that?"

Elena was a good listener, too, and Isabel found herself telling her sister about Spirit Week, but also about Kevin and Amanda and how she'd unintentionally gotten involved in their dramatic breakup.

Elena stopped stirring the soup and turned around to face her younger sister. "Oh, Isabel . . . sorry to have to tell you this, but that story will be all over school by tomorrow," she said matter of factly.

"I didn't tell anyone," Isabel said defensively.

"No, but those girls, Anna and Joline, obviously love to spread rumors." Elena put the lid back on the soup pot and asked, "Did I ever tell you about Karen Marsh, this girl in my class?"

Isabel shook her head. Elena rolled up two more burritos and set them on another tray that was almost ready to go into the oven before she started the story. Elena told Isabel that Karen had been this nice cheerleader, and she'd volunteered to help one of the football players with his homework. He'd been sick and needed updates on his assignments, and Karen was nice enough to give them to him and get him the right books so he could keep up with his class.

Someone at the school spread the rumor that Karen was only doing it to break up the football player and his girlfriend at the time. Even though Karen had a boyfriend that everyone knew about, the rumors flew all over, fueled by nasty IMs that were passed from one student to another.

Elena slid the second tray of burritos into the oven. "A lot of students just didn't understand that they were hurting Karen's feelings. They thought it was just a joke. 'We were just kidding,' " Elena mimicked in a singsong voice. "But her boyfriend thought the rumors were true, and he dumped her. Things got so out of control that Karen's mother went to the principal."

"That's so awful," Isabel said in an angry voice. "Karen wasn't even doing anything wrong—she was just trying to be nice!"

"And you were just trying to finish an art project and make a new friend," Elena came to her point. "But to people who love gossip, do you think that matters?"

Isabel started to feel a little sick inside. Hugging herself, she thought about how nasty the Queens of Mean could be, and how much they loved gossip. Were they going to make things so terrible for her that she would have to transfer to another school? What if people in her class started believing the rumors about her?

Elena set a plate in front of her with a fresh, hot burrito on it, but Isabel couldn't even look at it, much less take a bite. Her stomach was in knots. "Hey, what's the matter?" Elena wanted to know. "You were starving just a second ago. You don't like my burritos now?"

"Of course I do. I'm just not hungry anymore."

"I thought you couldn't wait for dinner!" Elena argued, her voice rising a little. She got upset when people didn't want to eat her food.

"Elena, it's not a big deal. I'll eat a little later, when Mama gets up. Right now I really just can't eat anything."

Elena looked crushed. "And all this time you always told me you loved my burritos," she said. "I didn't know you were just saying that to be nice."

Isabel groaned inside. Either she'd have to stuff herself on food she couldn't look at right now, or Elena wouldn't leave her alone. And all she could really think of was how much she wanted to talk to all the BSG and tell them what was happening. Thank goodness *they* were all her friends; they would help her make sense out of this mess.

CHAPTER

9

Reach for the Stars

ate afternoon, Charlotte was standing at her front door, trying desperately to get a leash on Marty, the cute little mutt the BSG had rescued from a garbage can. *Poor Avery*, sighed Charlotte as she tried to untangle the leash. Avery had wanted to keep Marty but couldn't have furry pets at home because of her mother's allergy. "But really, Marty," Charlotte said aloud to the little jumping ball before her, "you belong to all the BSG, and we love you to pieces, but I'm very glad that you live with me." She reached down to give the little dude, Avery's nickname for Marty, a pat. Avery usually walked Marty in the afternoons and spent as much time as she could with him, but with Spirit Week, everyone was busier than usual.

"Hang on, Marty," Charlotte begged the little dancing doggy. Trying to unknot the leash while leaning against the door and holding onto Marty's collar was proving to be difficult. "It'll be just a second."

When she pulled at a tight knot, the door flew open,

and Charlotte fell back inside the house. "Oh, dear," murmured her landlady, Miss Pierce. "Charlotte, dear, are you all right?"

Charlotte grabbed for the doorjamb and managed to steady herself just before she fell backward onto the floor. "Oh, hi, Miss Pierce," she managed. "Yes, I'm fine. I just can't seem to untangle this last knot."

"May I help? I love untying knots," offered Miss Pierce.

Charlotte handed the leash to her landlady and stared as Miss Pierce's delicate fingers loosened the knot in record time. Charlotte clapped her hands. "Thanks, Miss Pierce!"

Miss Pierce chuckled and said, "You're welcome, my dear. That last one was a real humdinger." Charlotte loved how Miss Pierce talked like someone out of an old-fashioned movie.

Charlotte clipped the leash to Marty's collar, and the pup yapped happily at the prospect of a walk in the park. When Charlotte looked away from Marty, she noticed that Miss Pierce, who almost never left the house, was actually dressed to go out–and she looked quite pretty.

Usually Miss Pierce's silvery white hair was rolled into a tight bun on top of her head, but today she had combed it down to her shoulders. She wore a pair of jeans, a warm pea coat, and a great red scarf thrown over her shoulder. "Wow, Miss Pierce," Charlotte exclaimed. "You look terrific!"

She was even more surprised when Miss Pierce answered, "Why, thank you, Charlotte. I was actually on my way to the park. If you and Marty are headed that way, I'll walk along with you."

"Yes–yes we are," Charlotte stammered. She couldn't remember the last time Miss Pierce had left her house; this must be a very special occasion!

Miss Pierce locked the front door carefully, and they set off toward the park. Charlotte wondered what could possibly have happened to pry Miss Pierce out of her house, but she didn't have to wonder very long; Miss Pierce explained as they walked. "You see, dear," she said, "I got an e-mail from an old astronomy professor of mine who used to teach at MIT." Miss Pierce kept astronomy equipment in her lower-floor apartment and also in a special part of the Tower, and she was constantly studying the stars. She was a real astronomer, and Charlotte just loved to hear her talk about the sky and all its wonders. Miss Pierce pushed her hands into her pockets and shivered a little. "My, it's getting cold."

"Yes, it is," Charlotte agreed politely. She thought maybe if Miss Pierce went out more often, she would feel more comfortable with the chilly weather!

But she wanted to hear more about Miss Pierce's errand, and when her landlady didn't say anything for a few moments, she prompted her, "You were saying something about your old astronomy professor?"

Miss Pierce had seemed lost in thought, but now she replied, "Oh, yes. He's a widower now and lives here in Brookline. He's retired from teaching, but he tutors college students because he loves the astronomy field so much. He asked if I'd meet him for a chat, to catch up on old times." She stopped for a minute and looked thoughtful, but didn't say any more.

"I think it's very nice that you're going out, Miss Pierce," Charlotte said carefully. She hoped Miss Pierce didn't think she was being nosy, but she wanted to encourage her to get out of the house more often. Being so reclusive was not a fun way to live for anyone, even someone as shy as Miss Pierce.

Miss Pierce looked up at the sky, in which a few clouds were drifting. "You know, Charlotte, I've been realizing lately that I can't spend my life cooped up at home. I'm an astronomer; I need to reach out toward the stars a little." Her eyes twinkled like stars as she added, "Besides, having you and Marty close by makes it easier to meet my old professor. If I don't like the way things are going, I can always use you two as an excuse to leave a little early."

Charlotte began to laugh. "It's always good to have a backup plan, Miss Pierce," she agreed. "But it sounds like you're going to enjoy this meeting; I don't think you have to worry too much."

Charlotte's thoughts turned to her own concern, the Spirit Week craziness at school. As they walked, she told Miss Pierce about the article she had planned to write for the *Sentinel* and how Jennifer had shot it down in the meeting. Like always, her landlady listened attentively as Charlotte gave her all the details. "So what do you plan to do instead?" she asked when Charlotte had finished. That was just like Miss Pierce. She was sympathetic when things went wrong, but she moved on quickly to uncover a solution. It must have been her scientific brain that made her so practical.

"I've been trying to figure out what spirit means to different people," she explained. "I thought that interviewing people about what spirit means to them would give me some good material."

"Now that's a very good question," Miss Pierce replied.

Why don't I ask her? Charlotte mused. Miss Pierce always gave helpful answers. Charlotte knew that Miss Pierce would give her a good answer about spirit, too. Without giving herself time to think any more about it, Charlotte asked boldly, "So what does spirit mean to you, Miss Pierce?"

Miss Pierce didn't hesitate. She looked up at the sky once more and said, "Why, spirit to me means reaching for the stars. One of my favorite quotes is by Ralph Waldo Emerson, who said, 'Hitch your wagon to a star.' With my career, it's obvious that I took it quite literally, but I believe it also means that you should reach for your dreams and push your limits until you are happy and successful."

"What a wonderful answer, Miss Pierce!" Charlotte cried. She quickly memorized it so she could write it down as soon as she got home.

They had reached the park. Miss Pierce stood looking around a little hesitantly, fiddling with the ends of her scarf. "Did your professor say where he was meeting you?" Charlotte prompted her.

"He said he'd find me," Miss Pierce said, her voice suddenly confident. "And I'm sure he will."

"Why don't you sit on a bench, then, and wait for him?" Charlotte suggested.

"Excellent idea. Thank you, dear. Have a nice walk. You too, Marty. And good luck with your article." Miss Pierce settled on a bench in clear view of the rest of the park and looked quite satisfied to wait in peace.

"Good luck, Miss Pierce. I hope you have a good time talking with your old friend. I think Marty needs a run today," Charlotte said, waving good-bye. Miss Pierce waved back at her, but Charlotte knew she was already a world away, thinking about her meeting.

Marty was pulling hard on the leash, and Charlotte looked ahead to see why: Marty had spotted some of his favorite doggy friends. Charlotte saw Louie the bulldog straining at his leash to get at Marty. Even better, she spotted La Fanny, the beautiful pink poodle who was sort of Marty's girlfriend, if dogs actually had girlfriends! And holding the end of La Fanny's leash was her owner, Ms. Razzberry Pink, whom Charlotte had met just a few months ago.

Ms. Razzberry Pink was definitely in the category of the unusual, because she had dyed pink hair and wore the color pink all the time. She had told Charlotte that it was important to dedicate your life to something, and so she had decided to dedicate her life to the color pink. She explained that pink made people happy, and so Razzberry figured that was a pretty good reason to open up her Think Pink boutique. Charlotte guessed that wearing all pink was a good advertisement for her business, too. Maeve was always saving up for the latest Think Pink item; this time it was an adorable pink velvet duffle with rhinestones. Ms. Pink was always friendly and interested in what was going on with Charlotte and the rest of the BSG, and that day she hailed her enthusiastically. "Hi, Charlotte! How are you and Marty?"

At that moment Charlotte lost control of Marty, who yanked the leash from the end of her fingers and ran off to play with his friends. Charlotte could see he wasn't interested in going anywhere dangerous, just running happily in circles and yipping at the top of his little doggy lungs, so she could spend some time talking to Ms. Pink instead of chasing him. She rubbed her sore fingers and said ruefully, "We're both fine, thanks for asking, Ms. Pink."

"How's school?" Ms. Razzberry Pink had gone to Abigail Adams Junior High herself, years before, so she always wanted to know about what was new there. "C'mon, sit down on this bench and tell me everything. I'll pretend that I'm young again."

Charlotte giggled. It was funny because Ms. Pink was actually not old at all . . . maybe twenty-nine or thirty. She sat down and started to tell Ms. Pink all about Spirit Week. She wasn't sure whether she could explain it very well, but once she started, Ms. Pink nodded knowingly. "Oh, yes. I loved Spirit Week. It was the first time I ever dyed my hair . . . pink, of course!"

Charlotte couldn't think how to answer that. Although she would never tell Miss Pink because she didn't want to hurt her feelings, she thought the pink hair was a little too much, and definitely not Charlotte's style. But Charlotte could see that Ms. Pink was excited about her Spirit Week story. So Charlotte, budding reporter that she was, encouraged her to go on. "Tell me all about it!"

"Oh, my, it really was something. Your Spirit Week sounds a lot like ours, with a dance and committees to join." Ms. Pink waited until she saw Charlotte's nod of confirmation before she went on. "Well, I decided my spirit was going to be about pink, so I dyed my hair and wore it that way the whole week. I knew people thought I was strange, but I didn't care. The pink hair was completely *me*, and it made me feel fabulous. Mrs. Fields was wonderful to me. I think she understood that I was one of those kids who was going to live outside of the box . . . and so I have."

"Really?" Charlotte asked. Whenever she talked to Razzberry, she forgot about the pink hair altogether and felt drawn into the Ms. Pink stories.

"Oh, yes, but you know something funny?" the store owner continued. "At the end of the week, when I made my speech about feeling the pink spirit, people clapped like crazy, and I realized I had actually said to the whole school what I really believed in my heart. It was a big moment for me, a real turning point. I think that was the first time," she said reflectively, "that I really felt good about expressing myself in my own way. And I made some good friends that week too. In fact, they're still my friends today." She stopped and turned to Charlotte. "Really, Spirit Week was very important in my life. I hope it'll be an amazing week for you, too."

It had taken Ms. Pink a long time to tell Charlotte the full story. When Charlotte looked at her watch, she realized that it was time to head home. "Thanks for sharing your Spirit Week story, Ms. Pink," she said, and she stood up to call Marty. Now that Charlotte had conducted interviews with the BSG, Miss Pierce, and Ms. Pink, she couldn't wait to get going on her article. *Jennifer's bad attitude is* not *going to get me down*, Charlotte resolved. Her angle for the article was really coming together, and she wanted to finalize a list of people who would be perfect to ask for their definition of spirit. She knew she wanted a quote from Mrs. Fields and some of her favorite seventh-grade teachers, and maybe she could even find a great quote from Abigail Adams, the second First Lady of the United States, for whom their school was named. "This article is going to be fantastic!" she whispered to herself. "I think it could be one of the best things I've ever done!"

"Marty, come!" she called. "Time to go home!" She pulled her coat more snugly around herself. It was starting to get bitterly cold. "Thanks so much, Ms. Pink," she said gratefully. "I can't wait to show my article to you when it's done."

"I'd love to read it, Charlotte," Ms. Pink answered, waving her pink-polished hand. "See you soon."

Marty trotted over to Charlotte obediently. His play time with his friends had tired him out enough that he was delighted to head home. Charlotte looked around for Miss Pierce. She'd left her on the bench right in the middle of the park and hadn't noticed her leaving, but Miss Pierce wasn't there now.

Well, it's getting cold, she told herself reasonably. *Maybe her professor arrived and they went inside for coffee. Probably to Montoya's Bakery.*

Charlotte walked to the edge of the park and started down Harvard Street, hoping she'd find Miss Pierce at Montoya's. But as she headed for the bakery, she saw two alarmingly familiar figures sauntering toward her. Oh, no! The Queens of Mean were headed right for her, looking pleased with themselves as usual. *Just what I need right now*, Charlotte thought.

The basketball was making its usual hollow thud in the driveway of the Madden house as Avery played a game of D-O-N-K-E-Y with her older brother, Scott. Taller than Avery by almost a foot, Scott also had a few more years of practice, since he was sixteen. But Avery was strong and accurate with her shots; she could usually count on winning at least half the D-O-N-K-E-Y games they played together.

Today, though, Avery was thinking as much about Spirit Week as about their game. As Scott dribbled the ball a couple of times and set up a shot, Avery said in a casual tone, "You know, I really think I can be the head of the sports committee."

Scott shot the ball and watched it swish neatly through the basket. "Another one for me," he said with satisfaction. "You've got D-O-N, and I've only got D . . . ha-ha!"

"Don't you think I could do a great job heading up the sports committee?" Avery said again, ignoring her brother's teasing. She wasn't in the mood for an all-out Madden battle, and she really wanted to know what her brother thought about going for the head spot.

But Scott wasn't too excited about the idea. "Oh,

I don't know," he said slowly. "Do you want to do it all by yourself? Why don't you work with a boy, like a co-chair or something? That way, you'd show everybody how the committees *and* the teams can be coed." He took another shot and watched it swish through the net. "Still only D for me."

Avery bristled. "Why does everyone think a boy should be running things? Why can't a girl do it herself?"

Scott shrugged. "You asked me, Ave. I just told you what I thought."

"Well, maybe I don't care what you think!" Avery shouted. She grabbed the basketball from Scott, even though it wasn't her turn, and started dribbling toward the basket. She was angry but just a little worried that Scott might be right, that having a girl and boy working together was really the right way to handle the sports committee. And because Avery was a little doubtful, she took out her frustration on the court.

"Hey, squirt!" Scott shouted. "This isn't one-on-one!" He chased her down by the basket, and Avery tried in vain to shoot the ball past him. But he was too tall and too good at guarding her, which was making her more and more frustrated!

Finally Avery did a quick pivot to get away from Scott and stood for a split second, aiming the ball at the basket, which was almost directly above her head.

Scott immediately jumped into her line of sight, and when she tried to pivot in another direction, he put his hand on her head to keep her from moving. "Scott, stop it!" Avery cried, trying to shake his hand off. "Foul! That's a foul!"

"This isn't a pickup game!" he shouted back. "We're playing D-O-N-K-E-Y, Avery! Stop being a baby—I just told you what I thought and you got mad at me!"

Avery was so furious that he was keeping her from the basket and now that he had called her a baby, she was determined to shoot no matter what. She tucked the ball under one arm and started pushing Scott away with her other arm. Scott grabbed her arm and wouldn't let go, no matter how hard she tried to pull away.

Finally, Avery gave up. She shoved the basketball hard into Scott's arms and started to jog off, mumbling under her breath. Scott threw the ball onto the grass. "Relax, Ave. I was just kidding," he said.

"Oh, sure!" Avery retorted. "Well, that's the second time I've heard that excuse today, and it's getting really old!"

Anyway, there was no point in wasting time with Scott. Avery knew she needed to go to her room and calm down. Then she would start thinking about a campaign that would guarantee she would be chosen to head up the sports committee. *What I need is a good slogan*, she thought.

Avery brainstormed as she climbed the steps to her room, and at her bedroom door, an idea flashed into her mind. She ran over to her desk, snatched a blank sheet of paper and wrote on it in bright red marker: SPORT SPIRIT —GIVE IT YOUR BEST!

She held the slogan at a distance, very satisfied with how it looked and sounded. *That ought to get people pumped*, she thought. *And it should be just what I need to prove that I'm the right person to run the sports committee!*

10

Without a Trail

Charlotte slowed her pace as she made her way down Harvard Street. The last thing she wanted was to run right into Anna and Joline, especially when she was worried about Miss Pierce. Where was Miss Pierce? It seemed kind of strange that she'd disappeared.

Even if I wasn't worried about Miss Pierce, I wouldn't want to run into the Queens of Mean, Charlotte admitted to herself. *They're rude enough to turn a day full of sunshine into a day of rain!*

But Anna and Joline seemed determined to run into Charlotte. "Oh, what a cute doggy!" Joline cried, kneeling down to pet Marty. Charlotte gritted her teeth and stopped; she couldn't get away from them without yanking poor Marty off his feet, and she refused to do that to the little dude, who was shamelessly wagging his tail at Joline.

"He is cute," Anna agreed, but she stayed on her feet and contented herself with making faces at Marty. And then, as though she had just noticed Charlotte, she said, "Oh, hey, Charlotte." Marty turned his doggy face up to Anna's and was wagging his tail winningly to grab her attention, but Anna kept her sharp eyes on Charlotte.

Joline was cooing to Marty. "You are such a beautiful dog, you sweet thing! Charlotte, what's his name again?"

"Marty," Charlotte said shortly. Everything about this meeting felt strange to her. She felt sure the Queens of Mean had something up their sleeves besides their arms!

"Maaaarty," Joline sang to the dog, stretching out the word and rubbing her cheek against his fur. "Marty, you are sooo darling!"

Marty, you are a such a flirt, Charlotte thought. *But you're wasting your time with these two. They're not sensitive enough to know how lovable you really are—they just want something from me, and they won't leave you alone 'til they get it!*

While Joline took Marty's paw and shook it, Anna said casually to Charlotte, "So, how's your friend Isabel?"

I smell a rat, Charlotte thought. *So that's why they're stopping me on the street!* Aloud, she said, "Oh, Isabel's great. Why do you ask?"

Anna just smiled tolerantly at her. "You'll find out tomorrow, I'm sure," she quipped. "C'mon, Joline."

Joline immediately got to her feet and followed her friend. Marty looked after Joline with a bewildered face as she and Anna traipsed down the street, giggling. Charlotte made a face after them, the kind of face you got when you bit into a sour lemon. Marty let out a couple of barks and spun around a few times, unable to understand that Joline had lost interest in him. *I knew it*, Charlotte said to herself.

"Don't worry, Marty, we still love you," she whispered to the disappointed pet.

"Charlotte, what is the big hurry up?" The question came from Yuri, the Russian grocer who often gave her lovely fresh apples in the mornings. "You have no time for Yuri and his fruit? These pears is from Chile. Beautiful fresh. Is best pears for cold weather."

"Oh, Yuri, you know I love your fruit. But I can't find Miss Pierce, and I'm beginning to worry about her."

"Cannot find? You lose her? She a whole person, how can you lose?" Yuri scratched his head as though he didn't quite understand.

"Well, sort of. We went to the park together, and when I was ready to leave she was gone. I'm hoping she just went to Montoya's for coffee and to warm up. But it seems kind of strange that she would just disappear."

Yuri thought for a minute. "I bring fruit Miss Pierce every week. Twice a week for long time, I bring her fruit. She never go out, Miss Pierce. Wait! She owe me money for last shipment. I not like to lose my good customers that owe me money!"

Charlotte couldn't help smiling, despite her anxiety about Miss Pierce. Yuri's grumpiness was kind of cute in its own way. "Hopefully she's just down the street at Montoya's. I'm sure everything's okay."

Yuri shook his head. "I was talking to my fruit here all afternoon. I would see her pass. She never come this way. She not at Montoya's."

Charlotte didn't say anything. Yuri tended to go back and forth from his outside stand to his shop to get more merchandise; she thought he could have been inside when Miss Pierce passed.

Yuri's weathered face was worried. "Here. You wait." He fumbled for a slip of paper and a pencil and wrote something down. "My e-mail address. You e-mail me later, yes? Tell me Miss Pierce is all good again, safe inside her house." He tried to seem offhand but couldn't quite manage it. Yuri was clearly concerned that Miss Pierce was missing. "Only so I can collect what she owe me, yes?"

Charlotte took the paper and smiled as she put it in her pocket. Yuri's e-mail address was appleman@yurifruit. com. She tried to smile up at Yuri, but she was getting more and more worried by the minute. She thought it was sweet that Yuri was worried about Miss Pierce, too, even if he tried to cover it up with all his talk about not losing good customers.

Charlotte continued on her way to Montoya's, hoping that she would be right and that Miss Pierce would be sitting at a table chatting with her old astronomy professor. *I'll just go in and look around*, she thought, *and then I'll . . . oh, no, I can't!*

She looked down unhappily at Marty trotting along next to her. She couldn't bring a dog into a bakery!

Well, then she'd have to see what she could spy from the outside. When she got to Montoya's, she leaned against the window and squinted. The bakery was well lit within, and Charlotte scanned the room from one side to the other. It wasn't very busy inside, making it easy to spot all the patrons.

Yuri was right. Miss Pierce wasn't there.

Suddenly, a face appeared on the other side of the window. *Oh, no!* It was Nick Montoya, a friend of Charlotte's who worked at the bakery to help out his family. He had just dropped off pastries and coffee to some college students, and after serving them, stood looking curiously at Charlotte.

Frozen in place with her face pressed flat against the window, Charlotte knew her features must be all smushed and distorted. She hoped she hadn't been drooling. That would have been too disgusting. Marty was jumping up and lapping at the window too. Nick tried to hold it in but he couldn't help it; he burst out laughing.

Charlotte jumped back from the window and turned a deep red. Could things get worse? She lost her landlady, and then Nick, who was so cute and really nice and one of her good friends, saw her having a Kodak moment against the bakery window!

Nick tapped on the window and pointed to the door, indicating that he'd meet her there. Charlotte hoped she could think of a good way to explain things, but as every step brought her closer to the door, she doubted it. It was just one more "perfect" Charlotte Ramsey moment, the kind that people would never let her forget and would end up under her yearbook picture.

"Hi, Char," Nick said with a smile, pushing open the door. "You coming in, or did you want to just hang out by the window?"

Charlotte broke into a smile. Nick was teasing her, but in a nice way. "Uh, no," Charlotte said. "No, I've got Marty with me."

"Oh. Well, are you looking for Isabel?"

Charlotte looked at him curiously. He was the second person that afternoon to ask about Isabel. Anna had mentioned her too, and Charlotte wondered what was going on. "No," she answered, "I'm looking for Miss Pierce, my landlady."

Nick frowned. "Miss Pierce? I thought she never left the house."

"She doesn't usually." Charlotte explained rapidly how Miss Pierce seemed to be lost and how Charlotte thought she might have come into Montoya's earlier with her friend.

Nick shook his head. "She hasn't been in here today. I've been on since school got out, and I haven't seen her. Actually, I don't think I've ever seen her in here."

Charlotte wondered whether Miss Pierce had just gone home. It was getting dark, and no one had seen her since Charlotte left her on the park bench more than an hour earlier. Even though Miss Pierce was an adult and didn't need to check in, Charlotte was getting a little worried. Miss Pierce wouldn't have left the park without telling her.

"Sorry, Char . . . I have to get back to work before my mother gets annoyed. We've been so busy today. Good luck finding her!" Nick called as he went back inside.

Time had slipped by and Charlotte realized that she had been gone much longer than she expected. It had gotten much colder, and it was almost completely dark. She said to Marty, "Come on, boy, we've got to get home fast. Dad'll be really worried about us."

She wrapped Marty's leash around her hand, whistled to him, and in a minute they were running up Harvard Street and around the corner onto Beacon, toward home.

But Charlotte's legs were much longer than poor Marty's, and he couldn't keep up with her. Besides, he was cold and hungry, just like Charlotte, and he began to yap unhappily. "All right, Marty." Charlotte paused and picked up the little dog. "I know you're too brave to be carried around, but we've got to get home fast. I'll give you all sorts of treats and hugs when we get there, and I'll wrap you in a warm soft towel so all the cold gets out of your fur. . . ."

She was trying to think of other treats to keep up Marty's spirits, when a car halted next to her. "Charlotte Ramsey," called a female voice. "What are you doing out alone in the dark?"

Charlotte looked over at the car. It was Officer Sue Moody, safety officer for all the Brookline schools, who lived around the corner from the Ramseys. "Are you okay?" Officer Moody asked. "Do you want a lift?"

"Oooh, yes!" Charlotte cried, her teeth chattering. "Thank you, Officer Moody! We're both freezing." She picked up a shivering Marty and climbed into the police car. She was lucky Officer Moody had stopped; it was getting darker by the minute, and by now her dad was probably worried sick about her.

Part Two
Surprise Endings

11

The Search Continues. . . .

When Officer Moody stopped the car in front of the rambling yellow Victorian house, the lights went on immediately in the downstairs hall. Charlotte bit her lip.

"Dad must have been looking out the window for me." Charlotte peered through the cruiser windows, glancing nervously at Officer Moody. She felt terrible that her father might be concerned. "You know, I was thinking about Miss Pierce so much, the time just got away from me. I never stopped to think that Dad might be worried about me. . . ."

As they stepped into the hallway, Mr. Ramsey came flying down the stairs. He was running so fast, he missed the last step, tripped, and fell forward onto all fours. Scrambling forward a few steps on his hands and knees, he struggled to regain his balance. The effect was one of a giant human bug looking for food. Charlotte began to giggle, and even Officer Moody had to hold back a smile.

Mr. Ramsey somehow managed to regain his balance and jumped up to wrap Charlotte in a big bear hug.

The klutz factor is obviously inherited, a bemused Charlotte thought.

"Charlotte!" Mr. Ramsey finally exclaimed. "Where have you been? Do you know how worried I was?"

Charlotte saw that Officer Moody's eyes were twinkling, but the police officer pressed her lips together and said with great seriousness, "Mr. Ramsey, Charlotte's been out looking for Miss Pierce. She seems to think that Miss Pierce may have—er—*gone missing*."

Mr. Ramsey's expression changed from relief to concern. Charlotte explained how she and Miss Pierce had walked to the park together, that Miss Pierce had arranged a meeting with her old astronomy professor, and then when Charlotte went looking for her, she suddenly seemed to have disappeared into thin air.

"Perhaps we should just check to make sure she didn't return to her apartment," Officer Moody suggested.

"I haven't heard a thing, and I've been home for hours." Mr. Ramsey looked doubtful. "Usually I hear her puttering around in the kitchen."

"Well, maybe she's come home but gotten sick," the officer suggested. "Perhaps we should check to see if she's there and needs medical attention."

"Good idea." Mr. Ramsey nodded.

Charlotte stared up at the safety officer. Did she really think Miss Pierce was ill?

When Officer Moody saw Charlotte's unhappy face, she said, "Most likely, that didn't happen, Charlotte! The truth is, Miss Pierce probably just got wrapped up in talking with her friend, and they decided to go somewhere to get a bite to eat and she lost track of time. Sometimes, you know, adults forget to tell people their plans, just the way kids do."

"That's just not like Miss Pierce." Charlotte shook her head. Miss Pierce was a scientist; she was *precise*. She had an excellent memory and wonderful manners. And since she was shy and reclusive most of the time, wandering off from the house and especially the neighborhood was a strange occurrence. No, thought Charlotte. It didn't add up.

But when they knocked on her apartment door and called out *"Miss Pierce!"* there was no answer. Mr. Ramsey dug out a spare key and cracked open the door. "Sapphire! It's Richard Ramsey," he said in a soft voice. The place was eerily quiet—no dramatic classical music playing, no sweet cookie smells coming from the kitchen. It was just an empty apartment . . . abandoned and lifeless. And that made Charlotte more worried than ever.

Officer Moody walked through the apartment, calling out for Miss Pierce. She checked all the closets, the bedroom, and the little landlady's study. Miss Pierce was simply nowhere to be found.

Reluctantly, the three closed and locked Miss Pierce's door and went upstairs to the Ramseys' warm, cozy apartment. "Did you receive any telephone messages or e-mails?" Officer Moody asked Mr. Ramsey.

He shook his head. "No phone messages at all. I checked when I came in." He went to his computer and quickly logged onto his e-mail account. "No. Nothing here that could be helpful. Just a few e-mails from a couple of my students."

Officer Moody took a small notebook out of her pocket and turned to Charlotte. "Did you ask anyone who was near Miss Pierce in the park if they'd seen anything suspicious?"

Charlotte's mouth dropped open. She hadn't even *thought* to ask anyone in the park.

Officer Moody saw her stricken face. "Don't worry, Charlotte. You've already done a lot of things right. You've eliminated some of the places where she could have been. There really wasn't much else you could have done on your own."

She turned to Mr. Ramsey. "You might check with Ferndale Hospital. That's the closest one. If there's been an accident near the park, she'd have been taken there."

Charlotte clasped her hands together as she watched her father dial the hospital number. Her eyes began to brim with tears. Miss Pierce truly understood her passion for the stars and her love of writing. Charlotte would be incredibly sad if something had happened to her quiet friend.

A few minutes later, her father put down the phone, shaking his head. "No one by the name of Sapphire Pierce was brought in today." He looked pointedly at Officer Moody. "Should we be worried, Sue?"

Officer Moody hesitated. "Well, 'concerned' might be a better word. Miss Pierce is a responsible adult. She's entitled to go off on her own. Maybe she's just gone to a long dinner with her old friend. She could come walking in here at any time."

But none of them really believed that. Even Marty's furry little body began to droop with discouragement.

Suddenly, there was a knock at the downstairs door. "Miss Pierce!" Charlotte cried. They all rushed down the stairs, but Charlotte was there first, even before Marty. Yipping happily, Marty acted as though he knew it was Miss Pierce at the door.

Not so.

When Charlotte yanked open the front door, there stood Yuri the grocer with a bag in one arm. "Hello! I bring you beautiful fruit to eat. Come, get me knife. I cut up all these fruit for a big salad. I bring for Miss Pierce."

Charlotte's face, which had been bright with hope, fell in disappointment. "Oh, hello, Yuri. It's . . . nice of you to bring that. But we don't know anything more about Miss Pierce. She's still missing."

"Yes, yes." Yuri had already managed to get inside the door, though Charlotte didn't remember inviting him in. He had an air of suppressed excitement about him, which Charlotte couldn't figure out. Yuri stepped forward and greeted the adults boisterously. "Hello, hello! Come. Yuri's here to cut you some of tasteful fruit."

Unsure what else to do, Mr. Ramsey led him upstairs to the kitchen, where Yuri commandeered the sink and unpacked a basket of plump strawberries, dark red cherries, oranges, and pears. He carefully washed them all in the sink, swiftly cut them up, and artfully arranged each slice on the small plates Charlotte brought out for him.

Wow, thought Charlotte. *Yuri's fruit display looks like something a TV chef would do.* She looked over at her father, who just shrugged his shoulders. He wasn't quite sure how to respond to the sudden bigheartedness of the bearish Russian grocer.

Once they were sitting, Yuri leaned on his elbows and dropped his voice confidentially. "You see me here now? I was most worried when Charlotte came today and tell me about Miss Pierce. She and I have tea and fruit together for years, every week. Not like lady to go off. Not like her to go out much! In fact, she never do go out!" He shook his head. "So I go to park myself. I walk up and down, tell people what she looks like—most beautiful lady—and ask if they see her." He held out his hand as though to describe Miss Pierce's size to a witness in the park.

Charlotte, biting into a luscious strawberry, suddenly had a thought that almost made her giggle out loud. *Yuri called her "most beautiful lady"! Could Yuri have a real crush on Miss Pierce?*

The others stared at Charlotte as she tried to stifle her giggle, only to end up hiccupping violently instead. Mr. Ramsey banged her on the back and Officer Moody went to the sink for some water. Finally, after one last enormous hiccup, she quieted down.

Yuri looked at Charlotte, his big bushy eyebrows furrowed with concern. "I finish important story now?"

Charlotte nodded vigorously. Her father and a skeptical Officer Moody waited for Yuri to continue.

Yuri described how he'd finally run into a group of young boys "on flying skates."

The others looked at each other. Finally Charlotte interpreted what he meant. "Flying . . . you mean skateboards? With wheels?"

Yuri pointed a finger at her and nodded. "But exactly! These boys skate and fly through the air. Yuri like to try it some day. I ask boys if they see her. They say yes; they see her today." Yuri pounded on the table again for emphasis.

Charlotte, Mr. Ramsey, and Officer Moody sat straight up. This was the first concrete news they'd heard of Miss Pierce in several hours. They all leaned forward, eager to hear the rest of Yuri's story.

But Yuri was one of those people who needed to tell every minute detail. He took his time describing the boys, their hair, where they were in the park. An impatient Mr. Ramsey finally prodded, "Yuri, please, what did they say?"

"Yes, yes, Yuri is getting to point." Clapping his big hands together in excitement, he revealed, "I ask skater boys where she go. They say she and gentleman get in big black car. They go with two men in black suits. The boys they say they sure these men are spies. Just like in movies. They say spies look around. They have . . . walkie tekkies. Yuri think skater boys are right."

"Spies?" Charlotte finally found her voice. "Real spies? How would they know?"

"They describe look of spies all right. In Russia I see same KGB spies . . . spies all the same." Yuri leaned forward conspiratorially and this time banged his spoon on the table. "They spy and look around. Not hard to find spies if you are looking like Yuri looks."

Officer Moody opened her mouth to ask a question, but Yuri was intent on finishing his story.

"Maybe you doubt Yuri. But is more. I tell you." Yuri hesitated to find the right word. "Boys say spies have gidgets."

"Gidgets?" A puzzled Charlotte looked over at her father.

"Yes. Gidgets. You know, techno gidgets. Boys say to me, 'Apple man, these is def spies. You stay far away from those dudes or they fly you away to Mars in a spaceship.'" Yuri looked at them appealingly. "Is all I know."

There was silence in the kitchen as the four of them struggled to understand Yuri's strange story. Charlotte was torn. Part of her wanted to laugh at Yuri's funny use of the word "gidgets," but she was too overtaken by one question. *Was it possible that Miss Pierce was kidnapped by real spies?* The thought made Charlotte feel queasy.

"Did the boys say there was a struggle, Yuri?" a suddenly stern Officer Moody asked.

"No, they don't say nothing about that," Yuri answered, his voice suddenly sad. Mr. Ramsey patted him on the shoulder. Yuri shook his head slowly. "What this mean then, people?" he asked no one in particular. "Is beautiful, small Miss Pierce a spy, too?"

CHAPTER

12

The Gossip Game

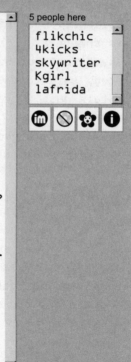

Chat Room: BSG

File Edit People View Help

flikchic: hey girls! BIG ANNOUNCEMENT! I'm gonna need all of your help
4kicks: what's the story??
flikchic: can't tell you now . . . online is 2 risky . . . I'll tell you in person. meet me at Montoya's b4 skool
Kgirl: just 1 clue. pleeease?
flikchic: nooo way! you'll see 2morrow. official BSG meeting . . . no one missing- no matter what!!!
skywriter: ugh speaking of missing, I have scary news
Kgirl: bad news? Not marty dog again
skywriter: no, not that . . .

5 people here

flikchic
4kicks
skywriter
Kgirl
lafrida

Miss Pierce kinda disappeared 2day

4kicks: WHAT????

skywriter: I took Marty 4 a walk and when I came back Miss Pierce was gone! I looked everywhere, embarrassed myself at Montoya's smushing my face against the window to see in!! :(

4kicks: again?

flikchic: poor Miss Pierce! is she OK???

skywriter: not sure. Officer Moody said to call the hospitals just in case and she wasn't there

Kgirl: that's good rite? she's OK at least, not hurt?

skywriter: I 4got to ask people at the park if they saw her leave. but Yuri talked to some sk8tr boys who said they saw an older woman and man getting into a big black car with 2 men dressed in black suits

Kgirl: whoa! could it b her?

5 people here

flikchic
4kicks
skywriter
Kgirl
lafrida

does Miss P know important
people?
4kicks: y would she b taking
off someplace? She hardly
even leaves the house. Seems
odd.
skywriter: u c what I mean?
MYSTERY
4kicks: maybe she's a secret
agent! maybe the men were
the men in black, like from
the alien movie!
lafrida: haha! I doubt it . . .
flikchic: welcome to the
convo, Iz! u have been so
quiet
lafrida: sorry
4kicks: yeah, seriously, Iz! u
OK?
lafrida: yes/no . . . complicated
skywriter: actually, something weird happened . . .
A&J AND Nick asked me if I
had seen u 2day
Kgirl: what's the deal?
lafrida: 2 words: Kevin Connors
flikchic: oooh tell now!

5 people here

flikchic
4kicks
skywriter
Kgirl
lafrida

Chat Room: BSG

File Edit People View Help

Kgirl: yeah-spill it, Iz. What's up??

lafrida: OK. I didn't want to talk bout this b/c it's private, but I know you guys won't tell any1 else. this Amanda-Kevin breakup is getting way out of control

flikchic: that explains how weird people were 2day

lafrida: I saw the whole thing when they were fighting in the art room. embarassing

skywriter: def totally know that feeling

lafrida: now people keep whispering around me. I even saw Amanda give me funny looks . . . and u heard what Chase said at lunch. I hope every1 knows this has nothing 2 do w/me

4kicks: y would they think u did anything? u guys are just friends . . . obv

lafrida: not sure, but something is def up! I feel like people are talking

5 people here

flikchic
4kicks
skywriter
Kgirl
lafrida

5 people here

flikchic
4kicks
skywriter
Kgirl
lafrida

about me. VERY WEIRD

skywriter: don't worry, Iz. no one has anything bad to say about u

flikchic: I don't know, Char . . . gossip at AAJH can get outta hand. it's not about Isabel . . . it's about who says what about who

lafrida: ick . . . so should I be worried??? Elena says could b bad news

Kgirl: no way, GF! u be confident-u did nothing wrong!

4kicks: anyone tries to mess, they'll have to answer to ME

skywriter: and me!

flikchic: smile, Iz! once my brilliant plan is set in motion everyone will b on ur side

lafrida: thanx BSG! U R the best!

Newsflash . . . It Was Kevanda–Now It's Kisabel

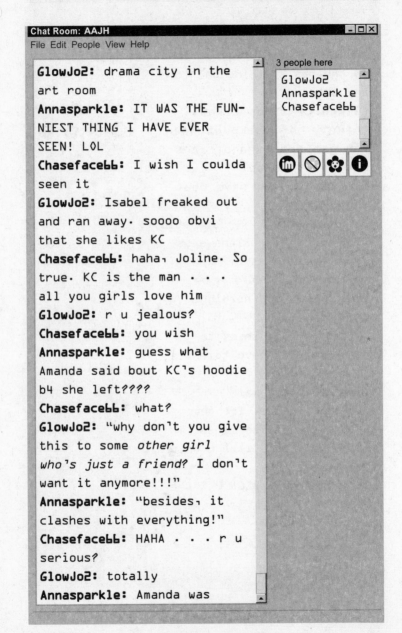

Chat Room: AAJH `- □ ×`

File Edit People View Help

GlowJo2: drama city in the art room

Annasparkle: IT WAS THE FUNNIEST THING I HAVE EVER SEEN! LOL

Chaseface66: I wish I coulda seen it

GlowJo2: Isabel freaked out and ran away. soooo obvi that she likes KC

Chaseface66: haha, Joline. So true. KC is the man . . . all you girls love him

GlowJo2: r u jealous?

Chaseface66: you wish

Annasparkle: guess what Amanda said bout KC's hoodie b4 she left????

Chaseface66: what?

GlowJo2: "why don't you give this to some *other girl who's just a friend*? I don't want it anymore!!!"

Annasparkle: "besides, it clashes with everything!"

Chaseface66: HAHA . . . r u serious?

GlowJo2: totally

Annasparkle: Amanda was

3 people here

GlowJo2
Annasparkle
Chaseface66

File Edit People View Help

3 people here

GlowJo2
Annasparkle
Chaseface66

soooo mad. she is waaay cooler than Isabel . . . do you think KC would EVER go for that BSG bird???
Chaseface66: no way . . . I'll make sure of it!
GlowJo2: really, how?
Chaseface66: we can have some fun . . . u know, a little joke
Annasparkle: I like the sound of this
GlowJo2: me 2!!!
Chaseface66: did Amanda really say his hoodie clashed w/everything??? that is 2 good
GlowJo2: TYPICAL. She wore the hoodie ALL THE TIME
Annasparkle: I laughed so hard, I was afraid KC would hear me. he didn't!!! phew . . .
GlowJo2: so what's the plan?
Chaseface66: well, every1 was talking about Kevanda . . . BUT NOW ISABEL IS TELLING EVERYONE THAT KEVIN IS ALL HERS (JK)

3 people here

Annasparkle: ahhh! gotcha
. . . soooo funny! KC will
freak out and dump bird girl
so fast she won't even know
what happened
GlowJo2: Kevanda . . .
hmm . . . how about Kisabel?
Annasparkle: hahaha! good 1,
glowjo2

GlowJo2
Annasparkle
Chaseface66

The Buzz Continues . . .

File Edit People View Help

6 people here

Annasparkle
Chaseface66
GlowJo2
DJsoxfan
Montoya33
Yurtmeister

Annasparkle: awesome bball practice 2day, kids . . . NOT!

GlowJo2: yeah seriously!!! staying after and running drills . . . not my idea of spirit week

Montoya33: our scrimmage was soooo bad

DJsoxfan: hey speak 4 urself. my game was totally on 2day

Montoya33: whatev, guys. we need to step it up if we want to win spirit week

Annasparkle: I'm w/u Nick

GlowJo2: totally

Chaseface66: me too . . . its 2 bad the girls keep getting in the way

Yurtmeister: oooh burn!

Annasparkle: hey, watch it, Chase!

GlowJo2: yeah what's that supposed to mean?

Chaseface66: not u 2! Kev was OFF 2day . . . a real mess out there

DJsoxfan: I noticed that 2. what's up with that?

Chaseface66: did u hear about the big breakup??

Annasparkle: I DID!

GlowJo2: OMG Yeah . . .

6 people here

Kevanda were totally like a MMIH

Montoya33: MMIH???

GlowJo2: match made in heaven, genius

Chaseface66: so how'd you hear about it, A?

Annasparkle: a little bird told me

Yurtmeister: I didn't know you were into bird watch-ing Anna! If only you had binoculars . . . you'd know EVERYTHING at AAJH

Annasparkle: HEY!!

Yurtmeister: haha, JK Anna. chill! U know UR my fave

Annasparkle: OK Yurt

Chaseface66: just so happens a little bird might be the source of the problem

DJsoxfan: huh? what do u mean?

Chaseface66: let's just say KC has been hanging out w some artsy girl . . . and Amanda's pretty angry

Montoya33: u mean Isabel Martinez?

Chaseface66: maybe

Annasparkle
Chaseface66
GlowJo2
DJsoxfan
Montoya33
Yurtmeister

Montoya33: no way. she's the last person who would cause a fight

Yurtmeister: yeah, she's my friend and she's cool, guys

Annasparkle: lol cool . . . now that's funny!

GlowJo2: hahaha yeah, good one, Yurtmeister.

Chaseface66: ummm I'd say u don't know your "friend" as well as u think Yurtman . . . she's causing all of KC's problems. U have NO idea

Annasparkle: Chase . . . call Kev and tell him to go sign on. I want to hear what he has 2 say!

GlowJo2: I want to know what Amanda thinks about this 2!

Annasparkle: should I call her?

Chaseface66: y not? this could b interesting

Annasparkle: I'll do the talking

GlowJo2: Anna can handle it!

DJsoxfan: dude this is

6 people here

Annasparkle
Chaseface66
GlowJo2
DJsoxfan
Montoya33
Yurtmeister

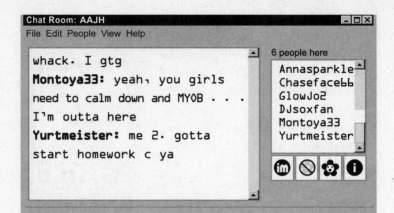

whack. I gtg
Montoya33: yeah, you girls
need to calm down and MYOB . . .
I'm outta here
Yurtmeister: me 2. gotta
start homework c ya

6 people here
Annasparkle
Chaseface66
GlowJo2
DJsoxfan
Montoya33
Yurtmeister

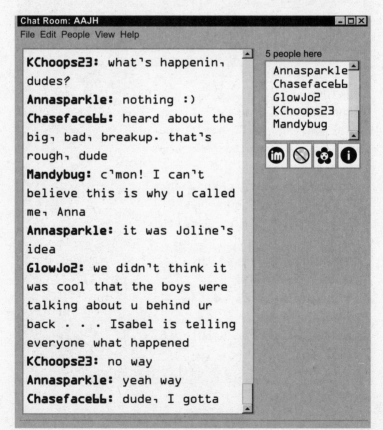

KChoops23: what's happenin,
dudes?
Annasparkle: nothing :)
Chaseface66: heard about the
big, bad, breakup. that's
rough, dude
Mandybug: c'mon! I can't
believe this is why u called
me, Anna
Annasparkle: it was Joline's
idea
GlowJo2: we didn't think it
was cool that the boys were
talking about u behind ur
back . . . Isabel is telling
everyone what happened
KChoops23: no way
Annasparkle: yeah way
Chaseface66: dude, I gotta

5 people here
Annasparkle
Chaseface66
GlowJo2
KChoops23
Mandybug

File Edit People View Help

warn you · · · girls are
flocking now that U R single
again · · · one bird-loving
weirdo comes to mind
KChoops23: what r u talking
about
Chaseface66: I'm just looking out for u, bro!
KChoops23: if u mean Isabel
· · · she is my friend
Mandybug: 4 someone who
"hates" drama u r doing an
awesome job of being the
center of it, Kevin
Annasparkle: no offense,
mandybug, but people r talking about you 2
Mandybug: r u kidding!!!?
Kevin, who did you tell???
Chaseface66: fight! fight!
fight!
KChoops23: WHAT! NO 1!
GlowJo2: I heard bird-nut
telling those lame BSG kids
at lunch
Annasparkle: she not only
paints birds · · · I guess
she squawks like one 2!!!
Mandybug: OMG, that snake! I

5 people here

Annasparkle
Chaseface66
GlowJo2
KChoops23
Mandybug

Chat Room: BSG `_ □ ✕`

File Edit People View Help

SAW her in the art room with
u Kevin. she must have heard
EVERYTHING

KChoops23: maybe u r rite
. . . but I thought she
seemed nice

Chaseface66: don't sweat it
bro . . . she is not worth
it! girls R so immature

Mandybug: speak for urself,
Chase

Chaseface66: hey, Amanda-
I am on team Kevanda! I
already made t-shirts

KChoops23: dude, this is
getting mad intense. I gtg

Annasparkle: me 2! Amanda,
conference call . . . u, me,
and Joline?

GlowJo2: totally

Mandybug: yeah, gimme 5 min

6 people here

Annasparkle
Chaseface66
GlowJo2
KChoops23
Mandybug

Kgirl: miss pierce home yet?

skywriter: no . . . they might call in the FBI

Kgirl: FBI? y?

skywriter: turns out man she met in park is some world famous astronomer

Kgirl: wow--this is too weird!

skywriter: tell me about it --fill you in on the details 2morrow

2 people here

Kgirl
skywriter

Summergirl: what's up, sis

Kgirl: drama-city in BSG world!

Summergirl: whoa, y?

Kgirl: everyone at skool is talking. Somehow Iz is in the middle

Summergirl: what? She's so sweet. How's she in the middle?

Kgirl: people think she likes this guy. It's really complicated

Summergirl: believe me. This stuff is sooo stupid. End

2 people here

Summergirl
Kgirl

2 people here

Summergirl
Kgirl

it b4 2 late

Kgirl: it's already 2 late

Summergirl: shortie, take it from an older sis who knows. NOT WORTH it

Kgirl: what?

Summergirl: GOSSIP = bad news, don't get involved

Kgirl: yeah . . . but some people think it's kind of exciting

Summergirl: 4 about a minute. then it's just hurtful

Kgirl: true. I'm getting sick of it. BTW, Char's landlady is missing

Summergirl: grandma's old friend?

Kgirl: yeah, Char is so worried

Summergirl: keep me posted on that one . . . that's important!

Kgirl: i will. c ya later

When she finished her homework, Isabel went online to see if any of the other BSG were still chatting. No luck. Nervous about all the gossip flying around about her, she decided to scroll down her buddy list and click on GLOWJO2.

If anyone was gossiping it would definitely be one of the Queens of Mean.

"Oh no," groaned Isabel. She could not believe what she was reading on Joline's away message:

```
A little bird told me that a total loser
with the initials I.M. (haha) is the cause
of the Kevanda breakup. Maybe I.M. should
wash the paint off her clothes and stop
being a turkey. Gobble gobble.
```

Isabel put her head in her hands. She could feel the tears welling up in her eyes. This was going to be way worse than she thought. *Everyone will think I am the evil break-up queen.*

Blabber,
blabber ...
Blabber,
blibber?
Blibber,
blabber!
Blib, blab, blobber?
Blib,
blab!
Blib, blab,
blob ... er?
I can't believe
she really said
that!

Isabel M.

13

"If You Can't Beat 'Em, Join 'Em"

Katani was the first of the BSG to arrive at Montoya's Bakery in the morning. Ever the budding business-woman, Katani tried to be on time for every appoint-ment, even if it was just with her friends. She was hoping she could grab a word with Isabel before the rest of the BSG arrived. Today she wore a gorgeous, multicolored velvet long-sleeved shirt she had designed and sewn with some help from her grandmother. She paired it with stretchy black leggings and a sparkling amber necklace . . . and, of course, her favorite black boots. But fashion wasn't on her mind this morning.

As Katani was studying the order board at the counter, she heard someone beside her say, "Hot tea, please. And a whole-grain sunshine muffin."

Katani glanced over. It was Betsy Fitzgerald, of course, Abigail Adams's resident type-A personality. Katani groaned inwardly. Betsy was actually okay when you talked to her about normal things, but the minute the conversation turned to school subjects, she became kind of obsessive. Katani moved away a step, hoping Betsy wouldn't notice her for awhile.

"You want butter on that muffin?" asked the girl behind the counter.

"No, thank you," Betsy declared. "That's very bad for your brain function, you know."

Katani looked at the counter girl, who was clearly used to Betsy's attitude, because she simply took Betsy's money, handed her a receipt and told her to wait; her tea and muffin would be ready shortly.

As Katani stepped up to place her own order, Betsy moved down the counter.

"Hi, Bets," Katani said. "Healthy breakfast, I see."

Betsy nodded very seriously. "I've been doing a lot of reading about how what you eat for breakfast affects your actions for the entire day," she pronounced.

Figures, Katani thought.

"And did you know," Betsy went on, "that eating healthy helps the brain perform significantly better?"

"Oh really?" Katani said. Betsy sounded like she was about forty years old. Katani wondered what Betsy would sound like when she *was* forty.

"Oh yes," Betsy went on. "Your neurons fire more smoothly when they've been primed with good breakfast foods. There've been lots of studies to prove it. Protein is best, of course, but unfortunately, Montoya's doesn't specialize in protein breakfasts."

Katani wondered why Betsy came to Montoya's at all, if that were the case. Everyone knew that the bakery specialized in big, beautiful pastries and delicious coffees, teas, and hot chocolates, not to mention Katani's favorite, chocolate biscotti.

Betsy went on, "So, I've been trying to eat healthier meals to improve my brain function, especially early in the morning. Our most important school tests are always administered in the mornings, you know."

"Good thinking, Bets," Katani said. "I'll bet you've already had some protein this morning, right?"

Betsy nodded. "Absolutely. I started my day with two hardboiled eggs," she explained. "That's the *best* source of protein."

"Good for you," Katani responded, glancing at her watch. Was Betsy a health food chef now, too?

"Can I help you?" the counter girl asked Katani. She looked like she was sick of listening to their conversation. Katani glanced at the menu again and made up her mind.

"Yes. I'd like a large hot chocolate with whipped cream and a toasted blueberry muffin." *Good to mix it up every once in a while. Maybe the blueberries will help my brain power,* Katani thought with a smile.

But it wasn't good enough for Betsy. She looked concerned. "Katani, I don't think that's going to work. That's too much sugar, not a good source of protein—"

"That'll be four twenty-five," the counter girl interrupted, eyebrows raised.

Katani paid for her breakfast and turned to Betsy.

"Well, tell you the truth, I've always felt the eighty/twenty formula worked best for me."

Betsy looked doubtful. "The what?"

"The eighty/twenty formula. My mom said that some doctors believe that if you eat healthy eighty percent of the time and exercise regularly, you can slip in a little treat the other twenty percent."

"I don't know about that." Betsy seemed skeptical. But Katani saw her glance at an appealing display of fresh, plump, chocolate-covered doughnuts covered with rainbow sprinkles.

"Works for me," Katani answered. "I eat pretty healthy for most of the week, but when I come to Montoya's, I know I'm going to eat something I really love. If I get something blah, it'll make me cranky, and when you get cranky at a really good bakery, it affects your neuron function for the rest of the day." Katani didn't know if that was true, but it could be, and she really thought that Betsy needed to lighten up a bit. She was so serious and focused all the time.

"Really?" Betsy seemed almost convinced by Katani's logic, but she wanted some proof. "Could you show me one of those studies?"

"Oh, I'd love to, Bets," Katani said as the counter girl set the tray with her hot chocolate and blueberry muffin in front of her, "but I can't remember where I read it. . . . I guess you'll just have to take my word for it. See you later."

She took her breakfast and started to head for the BSG's favorite table. Betsy looked over at the chocolate donuts again.

"You want one of those with your order?" asked the clerk.

"Uh . . . yes, thanks," Betsy finally decided, looking a little skeptical. "I think I'll save my muffin for later. I'm experimenting today. I'll see how it works." Betsy took a big bite of the donut as soon as the girl handed it to her.

The counter girl gave her a look that clearly said, *Early morning customers sure are bizarre sometimes!*

As Katani carried her tray toward the empty table in the corner, she saw Charlotte come through the door, looking worried. "Hey, Char!" she called. "Meet you at our table." She nodded at the corner window, which Maeve had once said was the perfect spot for the BSG to claim as their own. She observed that they would be able to see everyone who came in and out of Montoya's — which wasn't so important to Katani, but seemed to matter a lot to Maeve.

As Katani arranged her breakfast neatly in front of her, she remembered something that Nick had once said — that the worst thing about working in his family's bakery was having to clean up the messes people left behind. The kids were often the worst, and Nick dreaded seeing a group of kids come in for a snack, knowing they'd leave napkins and forks and other yucky stuff behind that he'd just have to wipe up. Nick was one of Charlotte's good friends, and for his sake, the girls made a special effort at Montoya's to leave their table as clean as it had been when they first sat down.

Katani had just taken the first bite of her warm muffin when Charlotte arrived at the table with a frozen hot chocolate and flaky crescent roll. Right behind her were

Avery, Isabel, and Maeve. Katani cringed when she saw that Isabel looked like she hadn't slept a wink. Katani had seen Joline's away message the night before and was hoping that Isabel hadn't. But Isabel's expression told Katani that she hadn't missed Joline's nasty little note.

Not wanting to make a big deal about it, Katani knelt down by Isabel's chair while the others were getting settled and gave her friend's shoulder a squeeze. "Don't worry, Iz. No one takes Anna and Joline seriously," she whispered.

Isabel smiled weakly at Katani but looked doubtful. "I hope you're right," she answered, "but I have a really bad feeling about this. I just can't talk about it right now. I've been thinking about it so much my brain hurts."

"Guys, I have the most amazing idea," Maeve jumped in right away. "I was trying to tell you about it yesterday, but things got a little out of hand."

"Hang on, Maeve," Katani interrupted her. "Any news about Miss Pierce, Char?"

Charlotte looked worried, and she seemed to be eating her breakfast without even looking at it or tasting it. "Officer Moody finally called in the police last night, and they searched Miss Pierce's apartment just like they do in the movies. You know, they even brought somebody over who hacked into her computer! They found her friend's address and went over to his house and then over to his office at MIT."

"And?" Katani probed. She'd forgotten all about her own breakfast.

Charlotte shook her head and took a deep breath,

looking at each girl in turn. "Nothing. Miss Pierce is really missing now. It's official."

Stunned, Katani, Isabel, and Maeve exchanged glances at this disturbing news. Their pastries lay untouched before them.

Avery, on the other hand, hadn't been paying attention. She had her head down and was eating busily, chewing her warm cinnamon roll. She took a long drink of her hot chocolate and swallowed, then asked, "Can I walk Marty later tonight, Char?"

Charlotte stared at her. Hadn't Avery heard anything she'd just said?

"Earth to Avery. Are you listening?" Katani asked. "Miss Pierce is *gone*. . . ."

"My dad said the police called in the FBI this morning," Charlotte murmured. Somehow this made her feel worse than anything else that had happened.

Avery's eyes widened. "The FBI! Whoa! Sorry, Char. I guess I didn't know that it was this serious. I figured she'd just show up or something."

"Maybe," Isabel suggested halfheartedly, "she just went on a trip. By herself . . . without telling anybody." But the more she said, the worse it seemed.

Charlotte shook her head despairingly. "She'd have told someone. Miss Pierce is too responsible to just drop everything and leave. Besides, she always checks in on Marty. She'd at least have left me a *note*." She thought back to their walk yesterday. "And she didn't look like she was planning on going anywhere except the park. In fact, I know she expected to come right home after visiting with her friend. None of this makes any sense. I am so, so scared." Seeing the stricken look on Charlotte's face filled her friends with worry.

"Have the police talked to the people she knows?" Katani asked. "I mean, shouldn't they talk to my grandma? She might know something." Mrs. Fields was one of Miss Pierce's best friends from when they were kids, and she made a habit of coming to tea at the house on Corey Road once a month.

"We gave them all the names we had," Charlotte answered. "I guess they'll check them out one by one."

Isabel suddenly ducked her head down. "What are you doing?" Katani asked. Then she noticed Anna and Joline strolling into Montoya's. "Oh. Those two." She saw the Queens of Mean give a snide look over at their table, and it seemed to be directed particularly at Isabel. Katani gave them the Kgirl stare and they quickly moved on to place their orders. "They're gone, Iz. You okay?"

Isabel shivered as she lifted her head and smoothed out her long black hair. "Those two are popping up everywhere!" She peeked over at Anna and Joline, who were waiting at the counter. They had their heads together like–*like birds*, Isabel thought. *They look just like blackbirds squawking at some poor little bluebird.*

The rest of the BSG were still thinking about Miss Pierce. Suddenly, Maeve clapped her hands. "I bet I know what happened to her. She's always studying those old stars and things. I bet aliens swooped down and picked her up off that park bench and took her away."

Avery burst out laughing. "Maeve, you've definitely

seen too many movies! Chill on the imagination, flikchic! Aliens? Ha!"

"Hey, it could happen," Maeve said defensively. "I saw a show on TV last week where people who really had been abducted by aliens talked about what happened to them."

"I saw that too," Isabel agreed. "But they also had doctors on afterward who said all these people who thought they were abducted had some sort of sickness that made them think it happened. I forget what they called it."

Charlotte, who had been frowning at her plate, raised her head and stared at Maeve. She stared very hard, deep in thought.

Finally, Maeve couldn't take it anymore. "What's the matter, Char? Do I have something in my teeth?"

Charlotte's face broke into her first smile of the morning. "Maeve, sometimes you are so brilliant I can't stand it," she exclaimed.

Nobody understood what Charlotte was getting at, and they all looked expectantly at her.

But Charlotte stood up immediately, grabbing her backpack. Her eyes were bright. "I've got to get to school right away," she said.

"What for?" Katani demanded. "What's all this about, anyway, Char?"

"I think I know who kidnapped Miss Pierce," Charlotte said confidently. She gave Maeve a big hug, picked up her tray, and started toward the garbage can.

"Hey, Char, come back, come back!" "Tell us what you think!" "Charlotte, at least wait for us!" A chorus of BSG protests called after Charlotte, but she was out the door in a matter of seconds.

"She thinks I'm brilliant." Maeve smiled brightly.

"I hope she has a good idea about Miss Pierce." Isabel crossed her fingers.

"What if she doesn't?" Avery demanded. "Or what if she's wrong? And what if something really bad has happened to Miss Pierce?"

"Be quiet, Avery. You don't want to even think that," Isabel said sharply.

Nobody wanted to think about that. They all took big gulps of their hot chocolates.

Katani was the first one to glance at the clock on the wall. "Listen, we've got to get going, or we'll all be late," she told the others. She started to collect their trash on her tray.

"Hey, guys, wait! Please! I have to talk to you about my idea! We don't have to be at school for another fifteen minutes." Maeve's eyes were pleading now, and no one wanted to hurt her feelings. Katani, Avery, and Isabel turned toward their friend.

A bubbly Maeve told them all about her idea for the dance, using the Birdland theme. "We can all put together amazing outfits, like the one Sarah was wearing in Ms. Ciara's class. Maybe we can even find some authentic stuff at a thrift shop or something. And the music, it's the best! It'll be so old-fashioned and romantic . . . totally different from what we usually do. Oh, and I thought Riley and the other Mustard Monkeys could dress in zoot suits! My dad's putting together some film clips I can use to show the dance committee what I want," she explained. "It's going to be so totally great! And I need you all on the committee, so you can vote for me to be the head of it!"

After Maeve finished her exuberant explanation, no one said anything.

Maeve looked around the table. She had expected everyone to be excited and jumping up and down, but nobody was doing anything like that. Isabel was doodling in her art notebook, Avery was bouncing in her seat impatiently and yawning with her mouth wide open, and Katani was looking impatiently at the clock. "Well?" Maeve asked finally.

Katani stirred. "Uh—Maeve, I don't know if I'm going to join any committees for Spirit Week. I have something else I'm doing, and I won't have time to—"

"Yeah, I can't be on it either," Avery abruptly broke in. "You can only pick one committee to be on, and I'm trying to be head of the sports committee, so I can't be on the dance committee too."

Maeve stared at her friends in dismay. "But if you don't join the committee, I won't get the votes I need to win! Isabel? Are you ditching me too?"

"No," Isabel said in a low voice. "I'll be glad to help out on the dance committee."

"But I can't win with just your vote and mine." Maeve pouted. "That's only two votes . . . and I'm sure a ton of people will vote for Betsy Fitzgerald!"

"Sorry I can't help, Maeve." Katani slung her backpack over her shoulder. "It's a good idea, though."

"Are you coming?" Isabel asked a minute later. Maeve

was still sitting in her chair, staring at her hot chocolate.

"No." Maeve flashed her a distracted smile. "I'll finish up and be right behind you. Don't wait for me," she added. There was a bright glint of an idea in her eye that no one noticed. They waved good-bye and reminded her they had only ten minutes left to get to class.

Maeve waited until all three BSG were out of sight before she picked up her hot chocolate and walked over to the table where Betsy Fitzgerald sat nibbling on her yummy-looking chocolate donut, her nose buried, as usual, in a thick textbook. "Hi, Betsy," she said casually. "Okay if I sit down?"

Betsy looked up. "Oh, hi, Maeve. Sure, you can sit, but I'm going to be leaving for school in two minutes."

"I know. Me too." Maeve sat down. She decided she didn't have time to work up to it subtly, so she just jumped right in. "I hear that you're thinking of heading the dance committee. Is that true?"

Betsy looked surprised and put down the textbook. "Yes. I know I could do a fantastic job. Plus, leadership positions look very impressive on college applications."

Maeve resisted the urge to roll her eyes and continued. "Well, I want to be the head of the dance committee too, and I have a great idea for a dance theme." She paused. "So I was thinking—how about we team up? We could both be heads of the committee, and with my idea and your organizational skills, we could make it the best dance ever. What do you think?"

Betsy seemed kind of intrigued but her watch alarm went off and she was up in a flash. She grabbed her backpack and slid in her textbook, double checking the contents of the bag and zipping it closed.

"I have to go, Maeve." Betsy said. "Want to come find me later and we can talk some more?"

"Definitely! I'll see you at school." Maeve waved good-bye to Betsy.

What is that old saying? Oh yeah, "If you can't beat 'em, join 'em." Maeve smiled as she rushed out of Montoya's at Betsy's heels, confident that she'd be able to convince Betsy that they would make the perfect team. *Charlotte was right,* Maeve thought. *I am brilliant!*

14

Jackpot

Charlotte started when Mrs. Fields called her name. She'd been deep in thought about Miss Pierce after asking Ms. Sahni if she could see the principal.

"I was going to call you to the office a little later." Mrs. Fields beckoned Charlotte into her office. "Have you heard anything?"

Charlotte told her quickly about Officer Moody, the police search, and the call to the FBI. "The FBI's Missing Persons Unit is working on it right now," she explained. Mrs. Fields sat back in her chair. She seemed stunned.

"So anyway, Mrs. Fields, I had an idea this morning. It might be stupid but . . ." Charlotte added quickly, "I mean, may I please use your computer for a minute?"

Mrs. Fields looked at her curiously. "If you think it will help. . . ."

"Thank you!" Charlotte went to her favorite search engine and typed in "Sapphire Pierce." She pressed Enter and held her breath.

There it was—pages of references to space shuttles, space debris, and other astronomical phenomena. Miss Pierce was quoted in all the articles and listed as a major authority. Her most recent article was just a month ago, and it was about an asteroid going off course.

Mrs. Fields stared at the screen in surprise. "Charlotte, you've hit the jackpot! I didn't realize Sapphire was still actively involved in the space program. I thought she just liked to monitor it from her computer in the comfort of her living room."

"I have a feeling," Charlotte said with a grin, "that we're soon going to find out Miss Pierce is involved with a lot of things none of us knows about."

Mrs. Fields matched Charlotte's grin with one of her own. "I have a feeling you're absolutely right."

Maeve caught up with Isabel on Harvard Street. Instead of walking at her usual energetic pace, Isabel had been lingering and peering into shop windows. Maeve had to urge her along.

When they finally got inside the school building, Maeve understood why Isabel had been so reluctant to hurry. A low but distinct buzz followed them all the way down the hall, along with many furtive pairs of eyes trying to watch them without seeming to. "I feel like I'm the star of a very bad after-school special," Isabel murmured to Maeve, just as someone walked by and mouthed, "Gobble Gobble."

"Naah, this is just what it feels like to be one of the most popular people in school," Maeve replied, trying to seem relaxed for Isabel's sake. She too was a little unnerved by all the stares and whispers. "It just means people know who you are." Maeve stopped at her locker and started to work the combination open.

"They didn't seem to care about who I was last week!" Isabel whispered.

Maeve shrugged and tossed her gym clothes into her locker. "Well, last week they hadn't heard that one of the coolest guys on campus broke up with his girlfriend for you."

"Maeve!" Isabel implored. "How can you say that? It's not true!" She walked partway down the hall to her own locker, which was by the eighth graders' lockers, and began to twirl the dial on the lock.

Maeve followed her friend. "Hey, Iz, I was just kidding. Anyway, maybe people are gossiping about you because someone like—oh, I don't know—let's say the Queens of Mean started a rotten rumor about you that everyone stupidly believes."

Isabel shuddered. "They did . . . they definitely did! And it's *so* mean! Did you see Joline's away message last night?"

"No, but I have a pretty good guess what it might've said." Maeve shook her head. "Don't worry, Izzy. By lunchtime something else will pop up, and everyone will forget all about you."

"I hope so. But it would have to be a pretty major rumor to take the heat off me. Joline's calling me and Kevin 'Kisabel.'"

"Maybe Anna McMasters will decide to elope with the Yurtmeister," Maeve joked. But inside she was worried. It sounded like Anna and Joline were up to no good.

Isabel laughed at Maeve's attempt at humor. It was pretty funny. No one in the seventh grade could understand what Henry Yurt saw in stuck-up Anna to make him so devoted to her, but he continued to be, even though Anna treated him like an annoying puppy. The BSG treated Marty way better than that! But Maeve's silly idea made Isabel laugh enough so that for a minute, she forgot the staring eyes of the other kids and their obvious whispers. Maeve could make anyone feel better.

They were late to homeroom by about a minute, which from Maeve's point of view made them early. Isabel thought at first that no one was going to notice her entrance, and she started breathing easier. The boys were huddled around Kevin's desk in the back and the Queens of Mean were sitting together on the radiator.

But then she heard it . . . that unusual hushed quiet and then the buzz. Was that a gobble she heard? *Not again!* Isabel thought with a sinking heart. *When is this ever going to end?*

"Everyone take your seats." Ms. R called the class to order. As Isabel started toward her seat, she caught a glimpse of Kevin looking unhappy and confused. The minute her eyes met his, he deliberately looked away.

Isabel felt as though he had slapped her. It didn't help when Chase snickered loudly.

Isabel slid into her seat. Charlotte was already there, sitting in front of her. She leaned back and said quietly, "Iz, is it me or is something happening here? Everyone is acting so weird!"

"Oh, I'd definitely say something's happening," Isabel

whispered back. She didn't want to go into detail because everyone was staring. But she wasn't going to pretend that something wasn't happening either.

"It's stupid gossip!" Isabel went on in a furious whisper. "It's so mean, and I am so sick—"

"Isabel, will you please pay attention!" Ms. R called. "I'm not going to ask you again."

Her face flushing a deep scarlet, Isabel sat back in her seat and said nothing further. Ms. R never had to speak to her before about talking in class. This was turning into a disaster of a day.

Anna and Joline were elbowing each other and laughing behind their hands. Chase was gobbling loudly, but he kept covering it up with coughs so Ms. R wouldn't yell at him. Just hearing Chase was enough to make Isabel feel sick to her stomach. She began to think that she should ask to go to the nurse's office. It would be so nice to escape to the quiet office and lie down until she felt a little better.

Ms. R opened her attendance book. "All right, everyone, here's the schedule. When I finish taking attendance, you can all head to your committee meetings. Remember, those are sports, dance, and community service." She began to read off the class list.

Avery and Maeve were clearly pumped. They were both smiling in their seats, eager to put their plans in action. Avery, as usual, was bouncing in her seat with nervous energy.

Katani, Charlotte, and Isabel felt a lot less enthusiastic. Spirit Week was not turning out to be the thrilling time they had anticipated after all.

After she had answered to her name, Isabel realized reluctantly that she couldn't go to the nurse's office and pretend to be sicker than she was. She had promised to help Maeve on the dance committee, and Maeve would need every vote to win the position she wanted so desperately. *I can't let her down*, Isabel told herself. *With everybody else in school against me, I need my real friends more than ever.*

She sighed. The very last thing she wanted to do today was face a room full of kids who were probably dying to gossip about her.

"Sports committee meets in this room!" Ms. R called out. "If you're joining that committee, stay here for your meeting. Dance committee meets in the art room."

Avery could hardly wait for the sports committee to assemble, and when it did she wasn't too surprised about the members from her homeroom: Pete Wexler, Nick, Josh, and Billy Trentini, Danny Pellegrino—who once made Isabel's life miserable because he liked her and wouldn't leave her alone—Joey Peppertone, and Julie Faber.

There was one surprise, though: Chelsea Briggs.

"Hey, Chelsea, you're joining the sports committee?" Avery asked. Maybe Chelsea was just snapping pictures for the *Sentinel*. She wasn't on any sports teams at school.

But Chelsea nodded. "I'll be a big help in the tug of war!" she announced with a grin. Avery couldn't believe it. Ever since Chelsea went on the school trip to Lake Rescue, she'd been a completely different girl. Not that she had morphed into a super-skinny type, but she was more fit than ever, and she seemed to be involved in all kinds of activities instead of spending most of her time alone. She ran and played pickup basketball with her brother and even started an after-school dance club with a bunch of other girls.

But Avery also didn't see one face she had expected to see. Where was Dillon? He'd been a huge jerk the day before, but he *had* apologized, and she thought he'd definitely want to be on the sports committee. Dillon was an awesome athlete, and Avery just assumed he'd help her out with her ideas.

He'll be here in a minute, she told herself. *He must have gotten held up or something.* But Dillon never showed up, and finally everyone started to settle down and the meeting began.

Quickly Avery raised her hand to be recognized. "I want to be the head of the sports committee," she announced. "I've got some great ideas about how to organize the games."

"A girl?" Pete Wexler said with disdain. "A *girl* running the sports committee? Are you dreamin', Madden, or what? Sports committees are men's work."

Avery jumped up. "Are you saying because I'm a girl I can't do a good job running games and sports for Spirit Week? I can't believe you, Wexler! Are you a caveman? That is so old school!"

"That's not the real problem," said Billy Trentini. He was looking embarrassed, and so was Josh. They were both looking at the ground, avoiding Avery's eyes.

"So, what's the real problem?" Avery challenged them. She was getting furious that no one seemed to want to hear her ideas; they were just shooting her down because she was a girl!

Danny Pellegrino was the one who finally said it. He cleared his throat and said, "Uh, Avery, the truth is, there's just too much drama around you."

"Drama?" Avery had no idea what he was talking about. She hoped it wasn't that silly incident with Dillon in the hall yesterday; if it was, she'd make sure everyone knew she and Dillon were over it and that it was no big deal.

Danny exchanged a look with Pete before he went on. "Look, you're friends with . . . uh . . . Isabel . . . and everyone at school is talking about what happened. We don't want to be caught up in all that. Spirit Week should just be about school spirit, and not about . . . uh, you know, gossip and rumors."

Avery's mouth dropped open. "Since when have I been spreading rumors?"

"That's not the point." Danny was looking more uncomfortable now, which was pretty funny, Avery thought, because when he was chasing Isabel through the museum a few months before, he was anything but shy and embarrassed! "Anyway, I nominate Pete and Nick as committee leaders." Nick looked very uncomfortable.

"I nominate Avery for committee leader," Chelsea said quickly.

"Okay, then," Billy said, looking relieved. "Let's vote on it. That's the only fair way to decide things."

Avery looked around the room. Julie and Chelsea were the only other girls. She was pretty sure how things were going to turn out, but what could she say? "No, let's not vote. I'll just be the dictator." That would *definitely* not be fair.

"Fine. Let's vote," Avery said, feeling defeated.

The vote went just the way Avery thought it would. Julie and Chelsea voted for Avery. The others voted for Pete and Nick. No surprise; the boys were elected.

Pete and Nick went to the front of the room to run the rest of the meeting. Avery said nothing; she just sat fuming in her seat. *Spirit Week is definitely not the highlight of the year*, she thought. *If this is spirit, it's for the birds!*

15

Uphill Dreams

aeve had no problem with any boys in the art room. That was because not one boy had elected to join the dance committee. The meeting consisted of about fifteen girls, including Maeve and Betsy. Unfortunately, Maeve's least favorite people of the moment, the Queens of Mean, showed up as well. Not a good sign, she sighed to herself.

Still, she finally had the audience she dreamed of to lay out her idea about a Birdland-themed dance. Maeve had walked to the meeting with Betsy and the two had made a pact to work together.

Maeve presented the idea to the girls in great detail: how they would transform the gym into a replica of the original Birdland (she showed them some photos she'd found on the Internet), and how the students could wear clothes resembling the old glamorous '40s costumes. "And we can do swing dancing, just like they used to," Maeve enthused, "and have the band dress up in zoot suits."

Maeve had really prepared for this presentation. She'd brought her father's movie posters, the CD he'd put together with old film clips, and even some hats and shoes she found in the Movie House costume bins. "Can you see how wonderful this is going to be?" she kept saying.

The room was silent when she finished her presentation. No one said anything for a whole minute, then Betsy jumped in. "Maeve and I thought we would team up to cochair this committee," she said, "and I've already organized a chart of how we can divide the work, so no one person has to do too much."

A few of the girls nodded at that, but the smiles and excitement Maeve had expected were nowhere to be seen. Did *anyone* like Birdland? She felt dejected. Suddenly, a tear began to well up in the corner of her eye. She quickly blinked it away.

"So, what do you think?" Maeve asked. Maybe everybody was just waiting to find the right words to express the fabulousness of the idea, she hoped.

Betsy didn't meet her eyes. "So, do you all agree that Maeve and I will cochair this committee?"

Joline snickered. "Well, nobody else seems to have any ideas, do they?"

Maeve looked around. It seemed like nobody did. She and Betsy would chair the committee, all right, but only because no one else cared enough, not because people loved her idea. She felt disappointed, but also a little relieved. Birdland was going to win out as the dance theme, if only because there was no competition!

Maeve tried to stir up some enthusiasm from the

rest of the group. "Who wants to get started working on the costumes?"

There was more silence. Betsy tried to help. "Well, how about decorations for the gym? Or getting the band? Who wants to work on what?"

The other girls looked at each other doubtfully. A few of them just shook their heads. The Queens of Mean just sat with fixed smiles, not looking at Maeve or Betsy or anyone else, and said nothing.

Maeve didn't understand what was going on. In her stomach she could feel a tinge of panic starting to spread. This wasn't supposed to happen! Everyone was supposed to love her idea, and Betsy was going to help her organize it so well that the dance would be the hit of Spirit Week—maybe even the hit of the year! *What's the deal? Why isn't anyone else excited about this, when it's obvious just how amazing it will be?*

Before Maeve could open her mouth to ask a question, the door burst open.

"We're here! Let the meeting begin!" proclaimed Chase Finley, with one of his typical obnoxious entrances. Behind him were Kevin, Dillon, and several others—the guys Maeve thought of as Kevin's posse—because they always hung around him and followed his lead.

I am not going to let them take control, Maeve determined silently. She said, in her best Ms. R tone, "We forgive you, don't we, girls, for your inexcusable tardiness, so if you will please just sit down we can finish up our plans for the dance."

"Finish?" Chase whooped. "Before you get *our* ideas? No way!"

By now he had managed to annoy and offend not just Maeve but every other girl in the room.

I am not going to let him see I'm mad, Maeve told herself. *Chase is just doing this to bug me.* She announced, "We've already decided on the dance theme. It's going to be Birdland, after that jazz music Ms. Ciara told us about. Everyone will wear forties and fifties clothes and do swing dancing, and the band will play old jazz music. It's going to be great."

The boys glanced at each other, then at the other, silent girls. Even Isabel was looking down at her desk, doodling, not meeting Maeve's excited eyes. "Doesn't look to me like anybody else is too excited about Birdland," Chase observed as he flapped his arms like a big bird. "That must be because you haven't heard our ideas yet. We saved the best for last!"

He slapped hands with a couple of the guys behind him. "And no offense, Maeve, but Birdland is lame! I mean, who else is even interested in birds? Have you noticed it's winter outside? No birds around at all—so why should we build our whole dance around them?"

The boys began to laugh, even Kevin, though he looked uncomfortable. Maeve felt suddenly completely deflated. *Is Chase right? Is my idea really lame?* She looked around the room. The boys were laughing at Chase's silly remarks, and the girls weren't making it any easier. They were studiously avoiding her. There didn't seem to be any enthusiasm at all for Birdland—even from the girls.

She decided to try one last time. "Birdland is a unique theme," she explained, addressing her remarks to Chase but hoping everyone else would listen. "It's glamorous and it's educational, too—we all get to learn a lot more about different kinds of music and dancing while we're having fun. And it's *different*. Nothing like Birdland has ever been done here before."

"Yeah, I wonder why!" Chase snorted. "Don't you get it, Maeve? Look at all these excited faces! Nobody wants to do Birdland but you. I conclude, then, that Birdland is for the birds!" Chase laughed at his own joke. "So, chill out already."

"Talk about lame, Chase," Maeve retorted. "That joke isn't even funny!"

"Hey, I'm not the one with the bad idea," Chase said, holding up his hands. "Now give us an idea we can get behind, and we'll be the best workers on this committee!"

"Yeah, I can really see that happening," Maeve said, feeling crushed. Her beautiful theme, her great idea, and all her work were going up in flames around her. What were they going to do for a theme if Birdland was suddenly out?

Betsy had obviously been thinking about that possibility. "I think we need to remember," she spoke up, "that this dance is honoring Spirit Week. So why not make our theme the Spirit of Abigail Adams?"

"That's not bad," Kevin began, but he was drowned out by Chase, who started a freewheeling cheer around the room, yelling, "Spirit, spirit, give me spirit! Hey, I've got it! Forget Spirit of Abigail Adams. We should do 'Under the Sea' as our theme!"

Chase looked so pleased with himself that Maeve

secretly wished he would fall flat on his face. But in a minute he was talking rapidly, all silliness abandoned, outlining how they could transform the gym into an ocean theme with painted murals and special lighting, and how the band could dress in shiny outfits that would resemble fish scales. Before Maeve or Betsy could say another word, the room was exploding with ideas and enthusiasm.

I might as well not even be here, Maeve thought as the meeting went on. *I wanted to be head of the dance committee and I guess I still am, but even Betsy didn't really like my idea.*

To her surprise, Isabel, who had been looking uncomfortable while Maeve talked about Birdland, was now sitting up straight in her seat, her eyes snapping. *Whoa, Isabel is angry*, Maeve thought. *It takes a lot to get Isabel mad, but boy, she's mad now!*

Isabel raised her hand, and as soon as Betsy pointed to her, she swung around in her seat to face Chase. "Chase, you're being mean," she began. "You get here late, after we discuss a very good idea for the dance, and without even listening to it, you decide you want to do something else! The least you can do is be quiet for a minute and let Maeve tell you about her idea."

"Hey!" Chase exclaimed. "You should take your own advice! You've been gossiping all over school, and now you're telling *us* to be quiet?"

He gave Kevin a high five.

Isabel felt like she was going to explode. "Excuse me," she said loudly, and the room went silent. She was the one that everyone was gossiping about, when she hadn't done anything to deserve it, and now she was being blamed for it?

Maeve saw the look in her eyes and quickly came over to her, followed by a couple of the other girls. "Don't say anything more, Izzy," she whispered under her breath.

"I am so . . . *fed up* with these guys!" Isabel answered. "None of this is my fault, and everyone's acting like it is!"

"I know," Maeve said soothingly. "We all know that, Iz. Chase is just being his ridiculous self, as usual. He loves picking on you because he knows it makes you mad. Don't let him see it's getting to you. C'mon, let's get this stupid meeting over with."

Isabel looked at her gratefully. "Thanks, Maeve. And— I'm sorry everyone's not more excited about Birdland."

"Let's forget it," Maeve said, feeling a giant lump in her throat. "The important thing is to agree on a theme we all can have fun with."

"Hey, you girls feel like doing some work here?" inquired Chase. "Because we have things to do, people to see . . . so let's get it over with and vote on the theme."

Betsy was able to restore order and organize a vote. But when the results were tallied, the boys' "Under the Sea" theme won by two votes. There were equal numbers of boys and girls in the room, so clearly some of the girls had voted for "Under the Sea." The vote was done anonymously, but Isabel and Maeve didn't have to look too far to figure out who had voted with the boys. Anna and Joline looked unusually pleased when the results were announced.

"I might have known they'd side with the guys," Isabel

muttered as she and Maeve packed up their stuff. "They spread gossip as much as Chase does."

"Lucky it's not some kind of germ that attacks every person who hears the gossip," Maeve commented. "Otherwise, the whole school would be infected with it by now! Abigail Adams could be wiped out with gossipitis!"

Isabel couldn't help laughing at that. Maeve always had a way of taking a rotten situation and making it funny, even when she herself was disappointed. Maeve really wanted to make the dance special, and she'd been more excited about it than anybody. *Why do things sometimes work out so wrong?*

But Maeve didn't want to think about Birdland anymore. She decided she would think about it later . . . with her dad. He was good at helping people when they were down in the dumps. Right now Maeve was wondering what the other BSG were up to. Katani had said she planned to do a community service project, and Avery was all about the sports committee. But where was Charlotte? She thought Charlotte would have joined the dance committee to support her. She hadn't heard that Charlotte was involved with any of the other groups. Where was that girl?

Spreading the News

Charlotte was sitting in the *Sentinel* office. She hadn't expected to be; she'd planned to join the dance committee and vote for Maeve. But just before she started for the art room, she was told to report to the newspaper office right away; Jennifer wanted to see her on an "urgent matter."

Now Jennifer was facing Charlotte, saying, "I've done

a lot of thinking about your proposal for a Spirit Week article, and it's just not going to work, Charlotte. Besides, we've got breaking news in school that I want you to cover. This Kevanda vs. Kisabel thing is a great story."

Charlotte winced. *Please, no. Not a story like that.* Jennifer obviously didn't recognize her discomfort because she kept going. "The gossip has spread around school, and it's all anyone's talking about. It would be a mistake to miss the opportunity. Let's call it 'Spirit Week . . . NOT!' See if you can get some interviews with all the people involved. And how about getting it in by, say, Friday?"

Charlotte was stunned. As *if* she'd write a gossip article about her own good friend for the whole school to see! What kind of person would do something like that? *Does Jennifer think I'm crazy?*

"Jennifer," she began, trying to keep her tone even, "I would never write an article like that for the *Sentinel*. The school paper is about news, not gossip. There are no facts to back up these rumors. Plus, you're asking me to write something that would really hurt Isabel Martinez, who happens to be a very good friend of mine. That's just plain wrong. I can't believe you would ask me to do something like that."

"I'm *asking* you," Jennifer shot back, "to act like a real reporter and keep your feelings out of this. That's what being a professional journalist is all about. Maybe in a few years you'll get the hang of it." Charlotte felt a flash of anger. Where did Jennifer get off talking to her like that? It's not like Jennifer was some award-winning reporter or anything, Charlotte thought angrily.

"Being a professional journalist means covering real news," Charlotte finally spoke up, "and not depending on stories about rumors and gossip, all of which are untrue. When you have a *real* news story for me, I'll be glad to cover it. You know that I'm a hard worker and will do as much as I can to make the *Sentinel* a great school paper. But it'd be easier for me to do my job if you would help me and give me good tips instead of ordering me around like I'm in third grade. In the meantime, you can forget about my covering this kind of junk."

And Charlotte walked out of the *Sentinel* office with her head held high, leaving Jennifer staring after her. Charlotte Ramsey was usually so meek. Jennifer was shocked, wondering what to do next.

When Maeve walked out of school, she was exhausted. She had spent the rest of her day trying to keep her chin up after the disappointment of the dance committee meeting. Now she couldn't keep the tears from welling up in her eyes. She'd wanted so badly to make Birdland the dance theme, and that was all over now. Her idea was clearly a dud. She squeezed her eyes shut for a minute, trying to push the tears back, and when she opened them, the first person she saw was her father, waving at her from the sidewalk.

"How'd it go, sweetheart?" he asked, giving her a big hug. "Was Birdland the hit of the day?"

"Dad," Maeve managed to say, burying her head in his sweater, "what're you doing here? Aren't you supposed to be at work?"

"Thought I'd pick you up and take you out for some pizza," he replied, beaming at her. "I called your mom to let her know. I just had to hear how the presentation went—I was thinking about you all day, and I couldn't wait 'til you got home to find out the news!"

Maeve tried to smile as her dad led her to his station wagon and opened the door for her. "Well," she said, "it didn't *exactly* go the way we planned it." Maeve felt terrible. She knew her dad would be almost as disappointed as she was about the way things had turned out.

"No?" Mr. Taylor listened while he drove, as Maeve explained about the reaction of the girls to her idea and then, worse, how the boys took over the meeting and forced everyone to accept their idea for Under the Sea. Finally, she finished, and a little sob forced its way out of her throat.

Her father sat quietly, saying nothing for a few minutes, but he reached over and gave her a pat on the shoulder.

"Maeve, honey," Mr. Taylor said softly when she stopped crying, "it mustn't have been easy to have the boys make fun of you and your idea without even taking the time to hear about it. But the fact is, you can never really tell how people will react. I thought Birdland was great. But the important question is, how do you feel about it?"

Maeve fumbled in her coat pocket for a tissue and wiped her eyes, thinking about what her dad had asked. How *did* she feel? "You know something, Dad," she said after a minute, "the funny thing is, I don't feel *totally* horrible because you know what I really think . . . that Birdland really *was* a pretty great idea, wasn't it?"

"It certainly was," her dad agreed immediately. "You had a fantastic presentation and it sounds like you did a great job with it. Just because the kids didn't want to do it, doesn't mean you were wrong. They simply couldn't recognize its greatness!"

Maeve smiled. "You know, that's just what I was thinking, too."

"Were you?" her dad teased. "How could you think at all with giant buckets of water coming out of your eyes?"

Maeve managed a weak smile. "Okay, I admit I was disappointed—for five minutes! But you know how big stars are—lots of drama and tears and then big smiles on the red carpet. Show business is tough, but you can't let anything get you down for long or you'll miss your next chance!"

"You are a real trooper, sweetheart, and that's what counts," her father reassured her. They drove the rest of the way with big smiles and dry eyes. Her father put on his CD from *The Music Man* and the two of them belted out "Seventy-Six Trombones." The car was practically rocking.

Isabel hurried home from school, eager to be in the one place where she could be sure no one was talking about her behind her back. At the door she got a big surprise . . . her mother, out of bed and smiling, was holding out her arms to her!

"*Mamacita!*" Isabel cried, using her pet name for her mother. "What are you doing out of bed? It's so good to see you up!"

"I feel wonderful today," her mother said. "And I love being able to meet both you and your sister at the door. *Como esta?*"

"How am I?" Isabel tried to laugh, but it came out as a choked-up sob. As she put down her backpack and took off her coat, she unraveled the whole story of the rumors and gossip that were following her around school. She tried to explain everything calmly, but her voice broke, and she had to hold back her tears. Her mother put her arms around her and patted her back soothingly, just as she had when Isabel was a very little girl. And as Isabel hugged her mother back, she felt better than she had in days.

"Let's have tea together, *bonita*," her mother said finally, patting Isabel's long dark hair. "Elena made some delicious cookies." She gave Isabel a grin. "We'll *test* a few, all right?" She moved around the kitchen, fixing things for an afternoon snack, and Isabel watched, happy to see her mother doing the things that had been an everyday routine before she got sick. Multiple sclerosis was weird that way. Sometimes you felt okay; sometimes you didn't.

When they sat down together in front of steaming mugs of tea, Mrs. Martinez nodded at the refrigerator, where several of Isabel's best bird cartoons were on display. "Look at those, Isabel. Those are *you*. Those are who you really are. That's what I hope you'll be thinking about, not silly gossip by unkind children who always have to make themselves feel better by saying mean things about other people. They have nothing to do with the *real* you,

Isabel. Your artwork, and your friends, and your school-work, and your family—those are the things that really define you. Do you see that?"

Isabel stirred a lump of sugar into her tea and squeezed lemon juice from the wedge her mother had placed on the saucer. She looked at her mother. "I think I forgot about all those things these last few days. It's hard not to care about what those kids say, but you're right. What they say doesn't matter. But it's embarrassing when everyone is talking about you behind your back."

Her mother held up her hand, squeezed two fingers together, and made the sign of something small. "Little minds with nothing better to think about. Silly little minds," she added for emphasis.

There was a bang at the front door, and then Elena was in the hallway, her teeth chattering. "Oooh, it's getting cold out there! We all need a good hot dinner tonight to warm us up."

"You're right," her mother said, "but there's no need for you to cook this evening. You need a break."

"Mama! I don't mind making dinner at all. I actually like doing the cooking."

"I know, honey, and I'm so glad you're able to help out when I'm not feeling well. But tonight I feel wonderful, and I think we should let someone else cook dinner—how about going out to Village Fare for pizza?"

"Oh! Yeah! Let's go to Village Fare!" Isabel suddenly felt as though the weight she'd been carrying for days was gone now. She didn't care who was at the pizza joint and who stared at her or talked about her. Her mother was so right. It had nothing to do with who she really was.

The three decided to walk the few blocks to Village Fare since Mrs. Martinez was feeling so well. Just as they were rounding the corner onto Washington Street, they heard a shout from behind them.

"Hey, wait up!" It was Avery, skateboarding at lightning speed to catch up with them.

"Ave! Uh, it's not exactly skateboarding weather. What are you doing?" Isabel asked.

Avery took off her helmet and unbuttoned her jacket a bit. "Just trying to get some boarding in before it snows or something. Where are you guys going?"

"Would you like to join us for pizza? We're headed to Village Fare," Mrs. Martinez said.

As if in response, Avery's stomach let out a loud *grumble*. "Oops!" She giggled and glanced at her watch. "Well, I have to be back in half an hour, but I can stop in for a slice. Thanks!"

Isabel, Elena, Mrs. Martinez, and Avery were just deciding on their order—a large pizza with half pepperoni, half sausage, and onions and green peppers on both sides—when they heard someone trying to get their attention. Turning around, they saw Maeve and her dad waving and grinning from a table in the corner.

"Come join us!" Mrs. Martinez called to them.

In a few minutes they'd pulled the tables together and soon everyone was chatting away excitedly. It was just what they all needed . . . a break from illness and school and gossip and the Queens of Mean, and a fun dinner with family and friends.

BSG Buzz

File Edit People View Help

skywriter: what happened 2 Spirit Week? it's def not what I thot it would b!

Kgirl: I'm with u. Seems this week is worse than regular skool. Spirit . . . NOT!

4kicks: u coming out 4 the games?

Kgirl: I'll try. doing a project 4 community service. we're doing a canned goods drive for a food pantry. might not have time 4 sports!

lafrida: sounds like a good project, K

Kgirl: I think so. anyway, no time 4 silly gossip

skywriter: u think we can get this week back on track? I hate what's happening 2 it

4kicks: I'm in

lafrida: me 2. would like 2 see real spirit at AAJH!

flikchic: rah, rah, rah!:-)

skywriter: I'm glad at least I said no 2 Jennifer about silly story 4 paper. gossip, not news! stay strong, IZ.

lafrida: thanks, Char

skywriter: even if u were not part of it, it still would b wrong 2 write about it!

5 people here

skywriter
Kgirl
flikchic
lafrida
4kicks

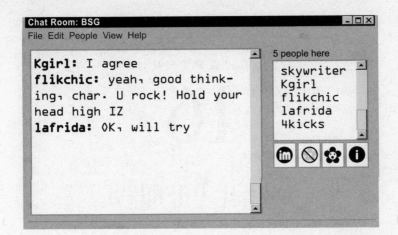

CHAPTER
16

Bench Warmers

Avery was already fantasizing about the Spirit Trophy before she even walked into school on Sports Day. She had dressed in her best warrior fashion—tying a blue bandana around her ponytail and smearing deep purple smudges of face paint under her eyes. Avery thought *that* made her look fierce. When they saw her, Anna and Joline burst out laughing. But then Dillon walked up behind Avery and draped his arm casually over her shoulder and asked, "What's so funny, girls? I hope it's not my buddy Avery, here."

The Queens of Mean stuck up their noses and walked away, identical pony tails swinging behind them. Avery and Dillon high-fived each other and, together, raced into class. Charlotte gave her fellow BSG a wave; she had saved a seat for Avery. After the homeroom teachers took attendance, the kids participating in Sports Day were dismissed to the gym. Avery was up out of her seat like a shot and down the hall. She was full of energy, ready to compete and confident that her group would crush their opponents!

Several of the boys in Ms. R's class had already made it to the gym and were warming up—passing the basketball back and forth across the court. The Yurtmeister was trying to lob the ball from half court into the net, but he kept coming up about ten feet short. Every time he missed, Yurt bowed low to the nonexistent crowd. One of the Trentinis shouted, "How many can you miss, dude?"

The boys gave a quick glance at Avery as she jogged in, and went back to passing the ball, practicing their shots, and joking around with each other. Nick and Dillon waved to her as they did sprints down the court, but no one else acknowledged her presence at all. *What am I, the invisible girl now?* Avery wondered. She followed Nick and Dillon with a few sprints and then hung around, waiting for one of the boys to pass the ball to her or call her name, but no one did.

This is so weird, Avery thought as she bent to tie her sneaker. She had never been left out of a sports event before, and this was a really important one: they were playing for the Spirit Trophy, which was awarded to the homeroom whose team won the most sporting events. Avery was determined that the trophy was going to be displayed in Ms. R's homeroom, but it would be hard to win if her teammates acted like she wasn't there!

Fortunately, Avery had brought something she thought would help unify the team. "Hey guys!" she called. "Come over here for a minute!"

The boys reluctantly slowed down their practice and wandered over to where she was standing. "Look what I have," Avery said, holding up a supply of blue bandanas just like the one she already wore. "If we all wear these with purple paint on our faces, we'll look like a super team. The other homerooms will be psyched out of their minds when they realize how serious we are about winning."

The boys took one look at her purple-rimmed eyes and snorted. "You really expect us to wear that?" Chase asked. "We'd look so dumb. The other teams would just *laugh* at us." Chase pumped his fist and said in a loud voice, "Purple paint. Rock it out, dudes." All the guys laughed—it was hard not to. Chase was a bit of an actor.

Avery had a really good comeback on the tip of her tongue, but at the last second she held herself back. This was supposed to be about team spirit, and starting an argument with Chase wasn't going to help one bit. "We should all wear the bandanas then," she said instead, trying to be patient. "Team unity and all that," she explained.

Chase hooted. "You mean I'd have to take off my lucky hat?" he asked, pointing to the Red Sox cap he wore backward on his head. The other boys nodded and stubbornly held onto their hats with both hands; none of them were giving them up, either.

Some of the girls who had joined Avery took a bandana and went to the restroom to smudge purple face paint under their eyes, but the boys ignored them and went back to their practice drills. Anna and Joline pointedly turned their backs and started practicing layups. *I can't believe them*, Avery fumed. She'd thought that her bandana idea was a no-brainer, and now it was completely ruined. Even Dillon and Nick said they didn't feel it would be right to dis the teammates who didn't want to wear anything.

When Ms. R's team finally assembled at the start of the game, there was nothing holding them together. The boys were in grungy sweats and T-shirts with various baseball caps, while the girls, minus Anna and Joline, stood out in blue bandanas and purple face paint. It made it look like the girls were on a totally separate team.

Whew, at least Katani showed up, Avery thought. *Even though she might be the worst player on the team, at least she's got the spirit, unlike* some *people I know*. Avery wouldn't even look at Dillon when he gave her a thumbs-up. If he wanted to stick with his secret society of boys, that was just fine with her. She went to sit by her friends.

Mrs. Fields made her way to the center of the basket-ball court to announce the rules of the competition. "We want this to be clean and fair," she stressed loudly. "Every-one who wants to play will get the chance. There will be two basketball games and a tug-of-war. The team that wins the most games will be declared the winner, and the Spirit Trophy will be displayed in that homeroom for the rest of the year. And while all students will receive T-shirts, the winning homeroom will get #1 Spirit Week T-shirts!"

The gym erupted into cheers. The Spirit Trophy was something that everyone could be proud of! And getting free T-shirts was like the cherry on the sundae!

Pete Wexler was team captain for Ms. R's class. He looked down at the scrap of paper in his hand and announced the starting lineup. "Here are the starters," he called. "Chase, Kevin, Dillon, Pete, and . . ." He squinted at the paper. Avery had stretched out and was ready to run out on the court. After all, she was one of the best basketball players in school, out of the girls *and* the boys! She knew she should be in the starting lineup; the team needed her skills to win the game.

Instead, Pete called out, ". . . and Riley. First team, out on the court! Let's win this one, men!"

Avery sat down, shock showing clearly in her face. "This is *outrageous*," she fumed to Julie Faber, another one of the best basketball players in the school. Pete's starting lineup was all boys. She watched them run out, high-fiving each other and bumping chests like teams did on TV. This game wasn't about spirit—it was about girls versus boys.

Ms. R's team was matched against Ms. Ciara's homeroom in the first round of basketball. Avery surveyed the scene and noticed that the lineup for Ms. Ciara's team had two girls on it. Their players were all wearing black T-shirts and green armbands, and they actually looked like a real team.

Avery, Chelsea, Katani, Isabel, Betsy, Anna, Joline, and the others sat on the bench watching and waiting for their chance. Pete was moving players in and out of the lineup strategically, watching the clock and calling for new people . . . but the boys just kept rotating in and out. They were getting tired, and some of them didn't have any of Avery or Julie's skills on the court. As the clock ticked on, the other girls looked over at Avery, who was now so furious she looked like she was going to explode. The color of her cheeks was rapidly coming close to the color of her purple war paint!

On the court, Pete was calling plays and seemed to be

totally focused on the game. "Number one!" he shouted as he caught a pass from Riley and started dribbling down the court. As Pete dribbled in place and paused for someone to get open, Nick shouted over to him, "Hey, Pete, how about putting Avery in? We could really use her. She hasn't played at all yet. Come on, dude."

"Later, man," Pete replied. "Get your head back in the game!"

Nick shrugged in Avery's direction as if to say "I tried," before he pivoted and caught a pass from Pete. Nick passed to Riley, who went in for a lay-up. The next time they paused for subs, Pete waved a hand at the bench and yelled, "Yurt, in!"

The Yurtmeister looked uncomfortable, which didn't happen very often to the class clown. "Come on, Pete," he said. "Put one of the girls in instead of me. Avery and Julie and Anna deserve a chance. They're some of the best players here."

The girls on the bench heard Henry and echoed him with a chorus of "Yeah, come on!" and "Let 'em play, Pete!" The boys on the court looked at Pete to see what he was going to do.

Pete looked back at "his boys." Avery called from the bench, "Come on, Pete, you have to give the girls a chance! We're supposed to be a team!"

Chase, who was reluctantly sitting on the bench after having played a full ten minutes, started laughing obnoxiously. "You're here to play? Oh, yeah? Girls don't know a thing about sports. Hey, Katani, who plays second base for the Red Sox?"

Katani, who was aware of Avery's frustration at sitting on the bench when she should have been on the court getting the job done, was sick of how the boys were treating her friend. She rolled her eyes at Chase. "What does that have to do with anything, Chase? In case you haven't noticed, we're playing *basketball* today."

It was a good point, but Avery also knew she could have answered Chase's question in her sleep. Anybody who was a Red Sox fan knew that second base was Dwight Molina territory. But Avery became even more infuriated when Chase began to taunt Katani for not answering his question. "You see why you're all sitting on the bench?" he said with a smirk. "What do girls know about sports? Zip, zero, nada. You better leave it to us, girls. We're gonna win this game!"

"Where are you from—dinosaurville?" retorted an affronted Katani. Chase actually blushed.

Good, thought Avery. *This boy-girl thing is getting way out of hand*. She high-fived Katani as she moved back to the bench.

When the buzzer sounded for the start of the second half, Pete gathered around him his "top" players, the original starting lineup. Avery, who hadn't sat out for an entire first half of any sports game since she had sprained her ankle earlier that year, was still on the bench . . . watching. Her jaw was clenched and she was trying to stare down Chase as he ran around the court.

With six seconds left in the second half, a foul was called on Charlie Meeker from Ms. Ciara's team. Ms. R's team was down by one point, so Pete had to make both foul shots in order to put his team ahead. The first shot went in cleanly with a *swish*. The second shot bounced from one side of the rim to the other and finally in the basket. When Ms. Ciara's team got the ball back, Charlie Meeker dribbled a few steps and then lobbed the ball down the court as the buzzer sounded, but the ball went nowhere near the net. Ms. R's team had won!

But no one on the bench felt in the least like celebrating. Chelsea, Avery, and the other girls just stared as the boys cavorted around the court, high-fiving each other and shouting at the top of their lungs. They were all pouring sweat from their exertions because most of them had played for at least half the game.

The girls who had waited on the bench the whole time still looked as fresh as though they'd just come out of the locker room.

Chelsea leaned over to Avery as the rest of the gym exploded in excitement. "Avery, no way is *this* what Spirit Week is supposed to be about."

"I so totally agree with you," Avery whispered back. "Anything would be better than this clown show!"

Ms. R was clapping enthusiastically for her winning team, along with other members of the class who were there to watch. She congratulated all the players, but Avery had had enough. She was not going to let the second game go the same way, that was for sure!

Avery jumped up and marched over to Ms. R, who was standing by the bleachers. She told Ms. R how she and the other girls had been shut out of the game entirely, even though they were ready and eager to play. "It's not fair,

Ms. R. I know Pete's the captain, but he's not playing by the rules of Spirit Week. Everyone is supposed to be able to play if they want to, and we all want a chance."

Ms. R looked at Avery's unhappy face and sighed. "I'm sorry this happened, Avery. I noticed that none of the girls were playing but I didn't realize it had gotten so out of hand. You'll get to play the next game, and so will anyone else who wants to. Leave it to me."

As the boys were stretching and resting up for the second game and Pete was writing the new lineup busily on his slip of paper, Ms. R strolled over to him. "Pete, why don't you just sit down? I'll put together the lineup for the next game. You've done enough work on this today."

Pete looked like she'd clobbered him with a goal post. "What? I'm the team captain, Ms. R; I'm the one who's supposed to decide on the lineups."

"Well, Pete, your lineup hasn't been quite fair. A lot of people are being left out, and that's going to change in this next game. Now please give the team list to me and I'll take over."

Pete had no choice but to hand over his paper to Ms. R. He looked over at the girls sitting on the bench and groaned. "We'll never win now. Ms. O'Reilly's class will dominate us. You let everyone play and it's good-bye, Spirit Trophy!"

"Sit down, Pete." Ms. R used her iciest tone. She meant business. "I *don't* want to have to ask you again. If you don't let everyone play, then it's good-bye *spirit*. You think about that. If you can't play fair, then I'm sure Mrs. Fields can think of something for you to do for her in the princi-pal's office."

Pete turned scarlet and slumped down on the bench. Ms. R glanced at his lineup sheet and then called, "All right, starting lineup for the second game: Avery, Isabel, Chase, Kevin, and Betsy."

Avery heard the groan from the boys as she, Isabel, and Betsy joined the group on the floor. She had never had a teammate be so negative about her in her whole life. She felt like crying right there. It was great that she would finally get to play, but what about the guys she'd always played with? Were they going to treat her differently now? Would they ever want to play with her again? Was Dillon even her friend anymore? Before, it had always been about who wanted to play and who had the skills. Now it was some stupid boys vs. girls thing that was ruining every-thing, and during Spirit Week, to top it off.

But it'll be better when we get out there, Avery told herself hopefully. *These guys know how I play. Once they're on the court with me, it'll be lots better.*

But it wasn't. To Avery's horror, as soon as the referee blew the whistle, Chase grabbed the ball from Betsy, who had gotten it on the jump ball, and passed to Kevin, who ran down court and aimed at the basket. Score two points for Ms. R's team.

From that point on, Chase and Kevin dominated the entire game. Not only would they not pass to the girls, but they wouldn't even look at them. It was as though they were playing all by themselves against Ms. O'Reilly's team!

Finally, Avery, frustrated that she and the other girls were being completely ignored, grabbed the ball while Chase was dribbling and started downcourt herself. She made a sweet basket, to thunderous applause from everyone on the bench. When Alexis Medley dribbled down the court, Avery stole the ball and dribbled back toward the basket, only to have the ball ripped away from her. Chase had stolen the ball, faked a jump shot, and passed the ball to Kevin. Avery, Betsy, and Isabel stood in shock. The boys were actually playing against them—their own teammates! Ms. O'Reilly's team glanced uneasily at each other and shrugged their shoulders as they chased the boys down the court.

After the game turned into five on two, Ms. O'Reilly's class gained a steady lead. Even though Ms. R tried to keep the playing time fair, the boys continued to ignore the girls on the court. Nick, Riley, and Yurt tried to keep it more balanced, but Pete, Dillon, Kevin, and Chase hogged the ball every time. When the game was over, the final score was Ms. O'Reilly's team 38, Ms. Rodriguez's team 27. Avery and the other girls sat back on the bench, bewildered and angry at how unfair everything had been, and the boys were sullen because they'd lost, despite their macho efforts.

By the time the tug-of-war started, Ms. Rodriguez's class had absolutely no team spirit whatsoever.

"All right, everyone, line up!" called Ms. R as the class sauntered over to the area where the tug-of-war rope was being positioned.

Isabel hung back with a group of girls, including Avery.

They all watched as the boys huddled together, talking about tug-of-war strategy. Except for Chase, most didn't look too happy with themselves or each other.

Now Isabel wondered if she should ask Kevin to talk to some of the other guys and get them to stop acting so selfish. She'd had such a nice talk with Kevin in the art room, before all the weirdness started, and she thought that when he was away from people like Chase, he could be a genuinely interesting and nice guy. Kevin was popular, too, and if he encouraged the boys to act a certain way, a lot of them would probably follow him.

She walked toward him as the class began to drift toward the tug-of-war rope. "Uh, Kevin?" she said tentatively. She didn't want to cause a scene or start the gossip chain all over again, but Kevin obviously wasn't paying attention. She tapped him lightly on the shoulder.

Uh-oh. Disaster movie in the making! Chase saw her.

"Oh, man, look at that!" he called loudly enough for everyone in the gym to hear. "Just what ole Kev needs, huh—a bird girl hanging on his shoulder!"

Isabel flushed an angry red, but Kevin never even turned around. He simply walked away from her, back toward Chase and the other boys. Isabel was furious. If that was how he was going to behave, then fine! *It's not my job to fix this whole Spirit Week disaster!* she thought as she whipped around and walked over to Avery and Katani.

By now it was obvious to everyone that the girls were fired up and channeling their anger to win the tug-of-war. Everyone, even the Queens of Mean, tied on the blue bandanas Avery had brought, and the purple paint on their faces made them look fierce and determined and almost like real warriors.

"Come on, everybody, let's *win* this thing!" Avery called. There was no way they could win the Spirit Trophy at this point; Ms. O'Reilly's homeroom had clinched it with two wins. But maybe they could still pull out some kind of class victory to save the sports competition from being a total bust.

Avery grabbed for the front of the rope nearest the center, but before her hands could lock securely on it, Chase jumped into the place ahead of her. "I should be up front," he announced loudly. "I'm stronger, so I should take the front spot to make sure we get the 'W,' and the other guys should be at the back to anchor it. Get out of the way, Avery. You saw what happened when the girls got into the basketball game. Can anybody spell *losers*?"

Ms. R was in his face before he finished the sentence. "What did you say, Chase?" she said quietly.

"Hey, c'mon, Ms. R, I'm just kidding!" he said, trying for a goofy grin. Avery wanted to knock that goofy grin off his face—if anything made them lose the second basketball game, it was Chase's pigheadedness and unwillingness to pass the ball to anyone other than his own buddies!

"The word loser is *not* allowed in my classroom, or anywhere in this school. Do you understand, Mr. Finley?" Ms. Rodriguez looked very stern. "I'll speak to you later. But now, the team should figure out what will be the best setup for tug-of-war, and I expect to see some girls in that lineup."

Most of the boys clustered in the front, with Henry Yurt flexing his not-too-impressive muscles at the end of the rope. "Okay, everyone get ready!" Ms. R announced, raising her arm in the air. "Let the tug-of-war . . . begin!" Ms. R lowered her arm to signal the start of the competition. Avery planted her feet and tugged the rope with all her might. Chelsea and Katani were in the back with Yurt, acting as anchors. Everyone strained to pull the rope, beads of sweat pouring down their faces. Since they'd all been arguing, they hadn't had time to set themselves up properly, and eventually the ropes slipped past the marker and the other team erupted into a cheer of victory.

When everyone poured back into Ms. R's classroom after the contest, Ms. R observed them for a few moments, pacing back and forth in front of the rows of seats. "It seems to me that many of you missed the entire point of Spirit Week," Ms. R finally said. "This week isn't about winning or losing as much as it's about being proud of your school and each other, and being part of a team." She gave Chase a pointed look. "Being a team player starts with respecting *everyone* on your team, female or male, and always thinking about how you can help them to be better and to have fun. There's no room for putting people down, and you can't use anyone else as an excuse for not winning. Everyone is in this together."

Chase looked down at his sneakers. He wasn't about to argue with Ms. R and get detention. But to Avery, it was obvious by the sour look on his face that he wasn't buying Ms. R's lesson.

Avery was listening intently to Ms. R, trying to overcome her own disappointment over Sports Day. What was there to look forward to now? Tomorrow was set aside for class skits honoring Spirit Week, and she didn't think her class stood a chance of pulling off a skit together.

But as she glanced around at the defeated-looking students, an idea popped into her head. Avery wasn't usually all that interested in skits and drama; that kind of stuff was Maeve's department. But a funny skit could be just the thing to help them get back the spirit they had lost.

Avery turned around to where Maeve, Charlotte, Isabel, and Katani were sitting. All four looked disillusioned. *Just wait until they hear my plan*, Avery thought. *It'll put smiles on their faces in no time.*

When the bell rang, Avery jumped up. "Maeve, I have a cool idea for the skits tomorrow." She grabbed Maeve's arm. "I think it could really help get our class spirit up again. But I need the help of a real pro, and you're the only one who can do it. Are you in?"

Maeve grinned. "Well, when you put it that way, how can I resist? A chance to practice my acting skills *and* help our team? Sounds like the best plan I've heard all day!"

"Yeah, we could sure use something to perk everyone up," Katani said, surveying the class as they packed up their bags. The room was unusually quiet, except for Chase, of course, who was talking loudly to Dillon about a new video game he had just gotten.

Katani wondered whether anything like this had happened in other years at Abigail Adams. There was one person she was certain would know the answer—and she made a mental note to ask her sister Candice that night.

File   Edit   People   View   Help

Kgirl: need help, sis!
Summergirl: what's up?
Kgirl: Spirit Week is turning out sooo bad
Summergirl: no way! Y?
Kgirl: the gossip thing with
Isabel is getting out of
control. now it's boys vs.
girls and 2 many people r
getting hurt. people keep
joking around but it's not
funny
Summergirl: oh yeah? Sorry 2
hear it. sometimes kids can
b really MEAN, esp. on the
Internet
Kgirl: yeah. big time. I
don't want Isabel or any1
else 2 get hurt. things
are getting out of control
online. ideas?
Summergirl: hmm . . . I just
heard this talk at school.
let me C if I can find the
flyer . . .
Kgirl: OK! I'll wait right
here . . .
Summergirl: here it is! it's
called a "no joke zone."

2 people here

Summergirl
Kgirl

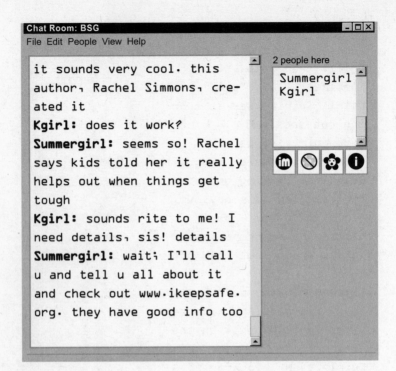

Chat Room: BSG

File Edit People View Help

it sounds very cool. this
author, Rachel Simmons, created it
Kgirl: does it work?
Summergirl: seems so! Rachel
says kids told her it really
helps out when things get
tough
Kgirl: sounds rite to me! I
need details, sis! details
Summergirl: wait; I'll call
u and tell u all about it
and check out www.ikeepsafe.
org. they have good info too

2 people here

Summergirl
Kgirl

3 KEEPS for Kids
From www.iKeepSafe.org
Keep Safe • Keep Away • Keep Telling

 I KEEP SAFE my personal information—all of it!
I never give my real name, address, phone number,
the name of my school, or a picture of myself
to anyone online.

 I KEEP AWAY from Internet strangers—no
matter what they tell me, because I have no
way of knowing who they really are.
I don't talk with them online, and I never
meet them face-to-face.

 I KEEP TELLING my parents about everything I
 see on the Internet—I always tell them or a
trusted adult when something makes me
uncomfortable.

CHAPTER

17

This Bird's a Quack

The next morning a very fidgety seventh grade sat in the auditorium. The buzz was upbeat despite the negative energy from yesterday's boys-versus-girls basketball fiasco. Everyone was waiting to watch the high school cheerleaders start Skits Day with a pep rally. The rally was a fun Spirit Week tradition, and the appearance of the high school champion cheerleaders was a big treat. "Who's got the pep? Who's got the spirit? Abigail Adams, so everybody cheer it! A-B-I-G-A-I-L! That's your name—uh-huh—so everybody yell! Gooooo, Abigail Adams! Gooooo, Abigail Adams! Whooo-hoooo!" The cheerleaders rocked the auditorium with their flips and amazing pyramids.

Maeve sat up straight watching their every move. Energetic and skilled, the cheerleaders were flipping across the stage like star performers. *Those uniforms are totally cute,* she marveled. *That red and white combo would look fabulous with my hair. When I'm in high school I'm so going to try out!* Maeve hesitated for a second. *Wait a minute,* she told herself. *Am I going to have time for cheer-leading and dance and theater? By the time I'm in high school I'll need to focus all of my extra time on my theater and movie career. I might not have time for cheerleading on top of that. Maybe they'll let me be an alternate or something. I just HAVE to have that uniform!*

Maeve sighed. Being totally committed to a future career in the entertainment industry did have its down-side!

She felt a tug on her sleeve. It was Charlotte, bringing her back down to earth. Mrs. Fields was applauding the cheerleaders and walking out to the microphone at the center of the stage. The principal would be introducing the skits soon, and Maeve knew that her group was up first. *Focus,* she reminded herself as she got up and followed the others backstage. *There are some things more important than cute uniforms!*

By the time Mrs. Fields was done, people couldn't wait to see the skits. There was nothing funnier than see-ing their classmates goof around on stage. Predictably, Ms. R's class hadn't been able to settle on one idea, so they were going to present two skits—one from the girls and one from the boys.

"And now," Mrs. Fields was saying, "I'm proud to announce the start of our Spirit Week skits. As you know, I've asked students to perform something that would show us what Spirit Week has meant to them. I expect all of you to give a great round of applause to anyone who has shown the "spirit" to get up and perform in front of their peers. She looked at a card in her hand. "The first group is 'Girl

Power . . . and Friends,' from Ms. Rodriguez's homeroom. Let's welcome Avery Madden to introduce them."

Avery walked out on stage, breathing hard. Her legs felt like jelly and she had clamped her hands to her side to keep them from shaking. Avery had *never* been this nervous before a big game. Performing on stage was definitely not her thing. She searched the crowd for Maeve. Sure, Avery had given speeches for student government in elementary school, and she'd gotten up in front of the entire seventh grade in the race for class president, but performance was a brand new thing for her. She hoped she wasn't getting what Maeve called "stage fright." She remembered Maeve saying that taking deep breaths helped to calm her down whenever she performed. Since Avery was breathing like she'd run a marathon, she figured she better employ Maeve's trick, and she began to take slow, smooth breaths. As she neared the microphone, Avery took one last big gulp of air, caught Maeve's wave out of the corner of her eye, and let the air out in a giant *whoosh*. Unfortunately, the audience heard her, and kids began to laugh. *Great. Just what I needed.* Her knees began to shake.

Mrs. Fields gave Avery a smile of encouragement and backed away from the microphone, which had been adjusted for her height. It was several inches too tall for Avery, so she quickly reached out to lower it, although she didn't know if it would make a difference. Right now, Avery was convinced that if she opened her mouth, the only thing that would come out would be a pitiful squeak—a sound more like Maeve's guinea pigs than a seventh-grade girl.

After fumbling for a few awkward seconds, Avery finally managed to slide the microphone down to the right level and lock it. Wiping her sweaty hands on her pants and glancing at her notecards, she faced the audience. "Our skit is called *Revenge of the Sports Martians from Planet Trogg* and it was inspired by this *particular* Spirit Week." She made sure to look directly at Chase Finley, who blinked at her but didn't even open his mouth to make one of his famous snide remarks. "Hope you like it—and hope you *get* it!" *Phew*, Avery thought. *I'm so glad that's over with.* She couldn't believe how exhausted she felt from saying those few words in front of an audience, and she had a newfound respect for Maeve. Being on stage was no joke!

As soon as she walked backstage, the curtain opened to show Maeve, Charlotte, Chelsea, Betsy, Katani, Isabel, and several other girls in Ms. R's class dressed in sports clothes. Each wore either baseball pants and a numbered T-shirt, basketball jerseys and baggy shorts, or tight white football pants with short-sleeved shirts bearing players' numbers. All of them were covered in dirt, as though they'd been playing hard. Each girl wore a sideways baseball cap on her head, and each girl's head hung down at a strange angle, as though it wasn't quite resting properly on her neck.

The girls had their arms stuck out and their eyes stared straight in front of them, like zombies. Their legs moved as though they were rubber, and they didn't seem to notice anything, not even each other, as they staggered around the stage.

Then several basketballs rolled across the stage, and

the staring eyes all lighted on them and began to chase after them. "Ball . . . ball . . ." murmured the zombies as they tried to stumble after the basketballs, almost falling over their own feet and bumping into each other without realizing it. "Must get ball . . . must pass to boy . . . must only pass to boy . . . must get ball and pass to boy."

As the zombies finally zeroed in on the slowing basketballs, Avery and a few other girls ran onto the stage. Unlike the zombies, the new cast members wore the bandanas and purple eye paint from the day before. They were clearly meant to be humans, because they called to each other and were graceful and alert as they tried to pick up the basketballs. But the zombies blocked them away from the basketballs, chanting "must get ball" and "must only pass to boy" while continuing to stare straight ahead.

When the girls tried to pull the basketballs away from the zombies, the zombies acted as though they were not there, while hilariously managing to stiffly throw the balls anywhere but the right place. Several basketballs went into the audience, some hit the other zombies. One even bounced lightly off Mrs. Fields, who tapped her foot in pretend annoyance.

Avery and the other girls shouted, "Throw it to me!" and "I'm open!" and "Over here, boys!" But the zombies ignored them and continued to throw the balls all over the place. Kids in the audience were loving it, calling out to the zombies to throw the balls in their direction.

The boys in Ms. R's class were beginning to whisper to each other and were shifting uncomfortably in their seats, but the rest of the auditorium was laughing.

Finally, Maeve, the head zombie, stumbled to the center of the stage. As the girls shouted, "Throw to me! I'm open, I'm open!" she acted as though all the noise was becoming too much for her. She put stiff zombie hands on her head, shook it from side to side, still staring, eyes wider than ever, and said loudly, "Must not pass. Must not . . . do not know why . . . " She seemed to be getting weaker by the second. " . . . Do not know . . . Red Sox . . . second baseman."

And with that, she stumbled one final time, fell face forward on the stage, and lay still.

Behind her, as though connected to their head zombie, the other zombies all wavered and began to teeter and fall, calling softly, "Red . . . Sox . . . second . . . baseman . . . second . . . baseman . . ." In two seconds, all the zombies lay still all over the stage.

The girls, led by Avery, looked down at the crumpled zombies and picked up the only basketball that was still on the stage. Soon they were running all over the "court," passing and shooting, shouting happily to each other when they fake-scored baskets. From the wings, the players were joined by Riley, Nick, and Dillon, who was back in Avery's good graces. They became part of the game right away, passing to the girls and to each other, dribbling around the court and setting up plays, shooting, and in general, acting like a real team.

Maeve raised her head slowly, as though with tremendous physical effort. She could "hear" the girls and boys playing well together. She focused her staring eyes on the game, then turned slowly to the audience and spoke the final line of the skit: "Zombie . . . make . . . big . . . mistake. Zombie want to play too." But it was too late, the game was over. Zombie Maeve staggered and her head dropped again, as though all the life had been drained out of her.

As the curtain closed, the audience laughed heartily and applauded until their hands stung. The Girl Power . . . and Friends skit was a big hit.

Mrs. Fields and Ms. Rodriguez both looked bemusedly at the boys from Ms. R's homeroom that were still in the audience. They seemed sheepish. Clearly, as Avery had hoped, they *got* it.

Mrs. Fields waited until the applause for the zombie skit died down and the actors returned to their seats before she introduced the next group. "And now let's all welcome Kevin Connors to introduce the 'Cool Dudes' of Ms. Rodriguez's class."

Kevin looked less sure of himself in front of a microphone than he did on the basketball court. He gripped the microphone tightly and said hesitantly, "And now, the Cool Dudes of Ms. R's homeroom in *The Blabber Birds*." Whistles and hoots emanated from the audience. "Bring it on!" someone shouted.

"Oh, no!" Charlotte whispered to Isabel. "I don't like the sound of this!"

Isabel said nothing, but clenched her hands together. Charlotte moved a little closer to Isabel and linked her arm through her friend's.

The curtain opened to show Chase dressed in a fluffy skirt (his gym shorts hanging down), oversized pink ballet shoes, and a white-feathered scarf and hat. He resembled one of the dodo birds from Sesame Street. Chase looked so completely silly that everyone began to crack up as soon as he flopped his way to the center of the stage.

Chase did a few classic yoga postures, with his arms floating in various poses above his head while he tried to stand on one leg, which provoked huge laughter from the audience. Even the teachers were laughing at his attempts at grace. Maeve had to admit that Chase did have really good comic timing.

Then Chase opened his mouth and began to sing—absurdly off-key—warbling like a bad opera singer and gesturing dramatically while still poised on one leg. His performance brought down the house. Ms. R was wiping tears from her eyes, and her face turned very red as she laughed helplessly. Even Charlotte and Isabel couldn't help but giggle . . . Chase looked like a complete dodo bird.

When he had finished his "song," another boy came out, dressed in basketball clothes and dribbling a ball, pretending to talk to Chase very seriously. Chase pretended to listen, his head attentively tilted toward the boy, and then, as the boy continued to mime a conversation, Chase flapped his wings and pretended to get upset.

Behind Chase came Derek Janner, one of the other boys who hung out with Kevin. He was wearing a trench raincoat belted across his waist and a hat pulled low over his eyes, which were hidden by sunglasses. But under the hat he had on a bird mask and wore a wig of long black hair. He carried a pair of large binoculars and trained them on the audience, watching them avidly and then turning to say something over his shoulder to another boy, who listened eagerly and then leaned forward and began to ask a series of eager questions: "Who? You don't mean it! You've got to be kidding! Where were they? When did you find out?"

Katani, Charlotte, Avery, Maeve, and Isabel sat in silence. None of them was laughing anymore. It was completely obvious . . . *Chase was impersonating Isabel and blaming the rumor on her!*

"Oh," Katani whispered to Charlotte, "this is so *not* funny! I don't ever want to speak to Chase Finley again. It's one thing to tease a whole group, but to single out one person in front of the whole school," and she looked at Isabel directly, "an innocent person . . . it's just plain mean. And what does this have to do with Spirit Week?"

"If you think about it," Charlotte whispered back, "this is *just* what Spirit Week has been about for our class this year. Gossip and rumors."

"But that's not what it's supposed to be about," Katani protested. "If my sister Candice could see this, she'd totally lose it! She loved Spirit Week at Abigail Adams, and she told me last night that it used to be the best week of the entire year. We are so not on the *right* track here."

"The question of the day is," Charlotte murmured, "how do we get back on the right track?"

The laughter of the audience, most of whom were still reacting to the boys dressing as bird girls, was building, and Chase was loving every minute of it. He fluttered around the stage, seeming to forget that he was supposed to be huddled in conversation with the boy next to him.

When the boy cleared his throat loudly, Chase kicked his heels in the air to a burst of giggles from the audience. They loved his skit, and he knew it.

The girls could almost see the wheels turning as Chase decided to improvise a new line. He stopped what he was doing, strode to the center of the stage, threw out his feathery chest, and said to Derek, "And you can just take your silly sweatshirt back . . . because it . . ." Chase was so excited by the audience response that he'd obviously forgotten whatever he planned to say. Finally, he burst out, "Because it will always remind me of you!"

Kevin, who had come back to the audience to sit down after introducing the skit, stiffened in his seat. His eyes flashed to the stage and then to Isabel, who was sitting at the end of the same row, her eyes glued on the stage in horror and disbelief.

Isabel's face was flame red. She wished she had never left Detroit. Her mother was doing better, so maybe they could move back *this* weekend.

Chase had just repeated almost exactly, word for word, what Amanda had said to Kevin that day in the art room, and he'd set up the skit as though Isabel was the gossip who repeated it all. But what Kevin knew, which Chase had apparently forgotten, was that *Isabel hadn't been in the room when Amanda was talking about the hoodie*. There was no way Isabel could have repeated anything like that to anyone, because she didn't even know it had happened. Someone else was framing her.

Kevin began to drip sweat. He felt like a total loser. Like everyone else, he had been led to believe that Isabel was behind all the rumors and gossip swirling around the breakup. He'd thought Isabel was pretty mean to spread his private life around school like that, when he'd liked and trusted her. But it was totally clear now that Isabel had had nothing to do with it; she *couldn't* have had anything to do with it. And yesterday she had even tried to talk to him—maybe to try to end all those dumb rumors—and he had just walked away and acted like she wasn't there. He hoped his mother and sisters never found out about this. They would be on his case forever!

He shook his head, thinking to himself, *What a bird brain! Oh, no*, he groaned at his own pun. *Enough about the birds.*

Kevin couldn't wait for the stupid skit to be over with. He had to find a way to apologize to Isabel. He hoped she would forgive him. As for Chase, he just might never speak to that phony dude again.

Luckily most of the audience had no idea about the truth of what had happened. They were just laughing at Chase's over-the-top acting style. Someone shouted, "Enough already!" Finally, to the relief of the BSG, Chase stopped the skit and took a long bow at center stage.

Anna and Joline were sitting with their mouths pursed. They weren't laughing at the skit either. Chase caught everyone's attention, and they were outraged. *They* should be the ones getting all the glory; none of this would have happened if it hadn't been for them. Anna whispered to Joline that she was never going to speak to Chase Finley again.

Katani leaned in to Avery. "Mark my words, Avery Madden. Chase just lost his best friend."

As the laughter and applause for Chase rose to a crescendo in the auditorium, Anna couldn't stand it anymore. All this applause should be for her, and no one would ever know that she had anything to do with it.

She stood up and shouted, "That's not the line, Chase, and you know it. That's not what she really said. It's 'Take back your hoodie, because it *clashes* with *everything* I own!'"

Instantly, there was a hushed silence in the auditorium. The boys onstage, even Chase, stopped cavorting and stood uncertainly. Amanda's mouth dropped open, and she and her friends turned in their seats to glare at Anna. Every member of the audience joined them, and then a low, insistent buzz began to rise from the seats.

Anna grew still as she saw the stares coming her way. This wasn't the applause she had been hoping for. These stares weren't friendly. They looked a lot, in fact, like the stares that had been directed at Isabel all week—cold and unfriendly. Anna tried to look away from them, but there were too many—even the teachers were staring at her. Joline yanked on Anna's sweater, "Sit down . . . you're going to get us into trouble."

Anna, realizing her predicament, tried to think of something else to say, but nothing came out of her mouth. She hastily sat down, and before she dropped her eyes to the floor, she saw that Kevin was looking at her with disgust.

"And it couldn't have happened to a nicer person," Katani whispered with a wink to Charlotte.

The buzz didn't stop. Anna whispered loudly to no

one in particular, "Look, you're making way too big a deal out of all this. The skit was a joke . . . the whole thing was a joke . . . I mean, we were *just kidding*." But the stares remained hard and cold on her face, and the whispers got louder. Finally, she became defensive. "Hey, can't anyone take a joke around here?"

Since no one seemed to be accepting her explanation, Anna worked her way out of her seat and hurried out of the auditorium. Queen of Mean no. 2, Joline, followed on her heels.

By now Mrs. Fields was up and rapping for order on the podium. She waved a hand at Chase and the others, directing them to return to their seats. Reluctantly, Chase left the stage.

Mrs. Fields looked sternly at the students. "I don't know what's going on here, but too many people seem to see something in this last skit that doesn't seem very funny to me at all. Spirit Week skits are supposed to be about what spirit means to you, and somehow I think this skit has completely missed the point. I won't be saying anymore about it, except to tell you that I find it very disturbing. I find it especially disturbing that many people were laughing at something that obviously is NOT funny and most likely has caused significant pain to someone in this room."

She said no more but rapped on the podium for quiet.

Charlotte glanced at Isabel. Thank goodness her friend had been publicly cleared of all the awful things other people thought she had done. Anna's jealous bid for attention had proved Isabel's innocence. Charlotte herself felt relieved. Isabel was safe. Now, if she only knew where Miss Pierce had gone to, life would be back to normal again.

She turned to say something to Katani, but Katani was no longer there.

Without a word to anyone, Katani had left in the middle of the assembly. Charlotte stared at the empty seat next to her.

What in the world is going on?

18

The Spirit Brigade

Suddenly Katani, looking confident, was standing by Mrs. Fields next to the microphone on the stage.

"Whoa, check it out!" Avery elbowed Charlotte, who looked up to see Katani onstage.

"What's she doing?" Isabel wondered.

"Whatever it is, Katani definitely doesn't have stage fright," Maeve whispered, filled with pride for her tall, stylish friend. Katani's outfit was to die for. The Kgirl had on her embroidered jeans with a shimmery orange top that sparkled as she walked across the stage.

The students quieted down when Mrs. Fields raised her hand, and Katani stepped forward to speak. "Hi, I'm Katani Summers and I'm in seventh grade in Ms. Rodriguez's homeroom. I'm here to ask you a question. Has anybody ever made a joke about you and then said, 'Just kidding!' . . . only it wasn't a funny joke at all—it was something that hurt? If so, raise your hand."

There was a long hesitation and a flutter of sound, and

then, slowly, most of the hands in the room went up.

Katani took a look around the auditorium, nodded, and continued. "It feels pretty awful, doesn't it? And somebody saying 'just kidding' doesn't make it better, even if that person says he or she is your BFF. The truth is, saying 'just kidding' is a great way to say something rotten to someone and then try to pretend you didn't mean it. It's like being able to get away with something, because you have this magic phrase that's supposed to make everything okay. And what makes it even worse is that whoever tells the joke expects you to laugh along with them, after they've said or done something really nasty. And if you don't laugh along, then you hear something like, 'Come on, dude. It was just a joke. Can't you take a joke?' Right?"

Katani paused and took a deep breath. Every eye in the auditorium was on her. "Well, from now on, nobody at Abigail Adams is allowed to be 'just kidding' about anything mean anymore." She paused again. "And because a lot of us got really carried away with this 'just kidding' stuff, Mrs. Fields is canceling the big Spirit Week dance."

There was a gasp from the audience.

Katani raised her hand. "Just kidding!"

The audience burst out laughing, but the laughter was uncomfortable, and people were glancing around at each other to see how other people in the room were taking the joke.

Katani nodded. "Not funny, right? Well, today I'm introducing a new magic phrase to Abigail Adams. Check it out: It's the 'No Joke Zone.' The next time someone makes a joke that's hurtful and says 'just kidding,' you can say, 'No joke zone.' And what that means is that what the person said is not okay with you. Whoever said 'just kidding' then says they're sorry for making the joke, and that's all. End of discussion. That way, a joke doesn't have a chance to hurt anyone, and you don't have to laugh along at something that you don't think is funny at all."

She waited until the auditorium quieted down. "For instance, tonight everybody has to write a five hundred–word essay on the 'No Joke Zone' for homework."

Maeve jumped out of her seat and yelled, "No joke zone!"

Katani nodded as the rest of the students laughed. "Right. Sorry. I should know better than to make a joke about something like that."

The students laughed again, and Katani went on. "You know, my older sisters went to school here and they told me all about how much they loved Spirit Week. They said that the students really got into it and competed with each other to show the most spirit for their school and their class. So I've been waiting what seems like forever for my own Spirit Week. And you know something? It's been a real letdown. This Spirit Week hasn't been fun at all. We've had spirit, all right, but it's been the wrong kind—mean e-mail and gossip and rumors and jokes about people who were totally innocent and who never had a chance to defend themselves. The truth is, we all got caught up in a weird kind of excitement this week . . . and some of us did some very uncool things."

The room was very quiet. Katani went on talking, look-ing into the faces of her classmates as she spoke. "Spirit

Week isn't about who's going out with who, or who broke up with who, or who gave back whose hoodie. This is supposed to be about students coming together, being part of this school and being proud of it, and showing especially what makes you happy and what makes you proud to be who you are.

"What makes me happy and proud is my family, my friends, and especially my sister Kelley. She's someone who really knows the meaning of Spirit Week, and she and her friends have put something special together that will show us all what makes her one of the most spirited people I know. Kelley taught me that you don't need a whole week to find what gives you spirit. Whatever helps you be you . . . *that's* what gives you spirit. So here," Katani stepped aside and held out her arm, "for the first time ever, is the Abigail Adams Spirit Brigade!"

The doors to the auditorium burst open, and in marched Kelley with a dozen other kids from her class, all smiling and excited. At the head of the group was the band teacher, and behind them came a small group of eighth-grade students playing instruments and shaking tambourines. Everyone could feel the *thump-thump-thump* of the drums vibrating through their seats. Band members were playing flutes, trumpets, trombones, and even a tuba. It was a real "spirit" parade!

Kelley and the students from her class marched around the auditorium with their favorite stuffed animals and a variety of posters. Some had movie posters; a few carried posters of their favorite sports teams; others held up posters they had drawn or painted themselves.

The group marched up onto the stage and stopped, standing in a straight line, their eyes shining. As the band teacher nodded, each one in turn stepped to the microphone and spoke into it. "Spirit is . . . the Red Sox!" shouted the first boy. He waved his fist in the air and yelled, "Go, Red Sox! Yeah!"

Avery jumped up and pumped her fist, "Red Sox forever!" she shouted. Charlotte, Maeve, and Isabel watched from their seats as the audience started to stir and respond to this unbridled enthusiasm.

A second student from Kelley's class walked proudly to the microphone. "*The Sound of Music* is my favorite movie!" she cried happily. There was applause from some of the girls in the audience. Maeve yelled out, "It's my favorite, too!" Charlotte and Isabel clapped enthusiastically. Charlotte was inspired. *I like this spirit.* She smiled as she grasped Isabel's hand.

Each student who had marched in the parade took a turn at the microphone, clutching his or her stuffed animal or poster or instrument and speaking about what gave them spirit. Some were funny; others touching. The applause from the audience got louder and louder.

"Everyone loves it!" Isabel exclaimed, looking at the students who had been sullen and silent just a short time ago.

Charlotte nodded. "I guess everyone's realizing that it's really more fun to be excited than to put people down," she surmised. Charlotte had already learned a lot about "negative spirit" during this week at Abigail Adams . . . and she was glad it was almost over.

The last student at the microphone was Kelley. Clutching Mr. Bear tightly, she stood at the microphone. "My spirit is . . . Mr. Bear." She gave him a squeeze and held him up proudly for everyone to see. Everyone clapped, but Kelley shook her head and yelled, "I'm not finished yet! I have more spirit!" and looked at her sister. "My sister Katani." Katani smiled at her and waved. "And my best friend, my very best friend, Charlotte." She looked into the audience until she caught Charlotte's eye. Then she gave a little bow and walked off.

To the *thump-thump-thump* of the drums and the brass instruments playing a lively tune, Kelley's class marched onto the stage for one final round of applause. The eighth graders who had joined the parade each grabbed the hand of a student from Kelley's class and raised it in the air. They had electrified the other students and completely lifted everyone's sinking spirits. There were whistles and hoots and a few tears from some of the teachers.

Charlotte was deeply touched that Kelley had mentioned her, and now she blinked away a little tear. Avery gave her a bewildered look. Charlotte just shrugged. "Kelley is so cool," she mumbled as she clapped with the rest of the audience.

Avery nodded. "Those kids totally turned things around today! I just wish they'd had their march before Sports Day," Avery shouted over the applause.

"At least the dance'll be better," Maeve added, leaning forward to talk to them.

Charlotte shook her head. "How can it be?"

Maeve looked puzzled. "Well, everyone already has lots more spirit. What do you mean?"

"Maeve, have you forgotten? There's one little problem with the dance. The boys voted in the Under the Sea theme, but no one's done any work on it yet. Everyone's been too wrapped up in all the other stuff that's happened."

They all looked at each other. Charlotte was so right. Even seeing Ms. R hurry Chase Finley out of the auditorium didn't make them feel better. Even Kevin's apologetic glance at Isabel didn't make everything okay again. Spirit Week wouldn't really be saved unless the big dance was a special night to remember.

19

A Hero's Welcome

Charlotte was still thinking hard about the dance and how they could possibly salvage it when she got home from school and went up to her room. She had to finish her *Sentinel* article today if it was to be published in the next issue of the paper. Of course, Jennifer would probably hate it and pull it out of the issue. "Oh well," Charlotte said with a sigh. Writing the story had made Charlotte feel good, even if no one else would see it.

Quickly, she turned on her computer to write the last paragraphs of the article and to see if maybe there was any news about Miss Pierce. The computer booted up and Charlotte clicked on her Internet icon; she had set it to the homepage of the *Boston Globe* so she could check out interesting headlines whenever she logged onto her computer.

Today, however, when the *Globe's* homepage loaded and Charlotte glanced at it, she stopped cold. Her eyes widened. Then she ran out of her room and shouted at the top of her lungs, "DAD! DAAAAD! Come up here right now! Hurry!"

Her father took the stairs three at a time. Charlotte's cries had frightened him badly. "What is it? What's wrong? Are you okay?" he panted as he tore into her room.

Charlotte pointed a shaking finger at the computer screen. "Look! Do you believe this? I was right! Can you believe it?!"

They both stared at the screen. There, in a huge photo spread at the center of the *Globe* homepage, was Miss Pierce, standing next to an elderly gentleman in the *Oval Office* and shaking hands with none other than the *President of the United States*!!

Charlotte and her dad began to read. . . .

❧ . . . . ❧

RETIRED SCIENTISTS AVERT
SPACE SHUTTLE DISASTER

To friends and neighbors around Beacon Street, Sapphire Pierce is a sweet, quiet lady who lives on Corey Hill and generally keeps to herself. Miss Pierce remarked, "I've always loved looking at the stars . . . perhaps because things here on Earth are often overwhelming to me. Little things—like going to buy fruit or groceries—are difficult for me." But little did Sapphire Pierce know that everything was about to change.

Enter Dr. Peaker Townsend. When Dr. Townsend was a professor at MIT ten years ago, he published three books and over twenty articles about the increasingly concerning situation plaguing the universe today known as "space debris." Lately Dr.

Townsend has been spending his time "just hitting a bucket of balls, eating ham sandwiches, and playing with my grandchildren." When it came to the issue of space debris, Dr. Townsend stated, "I thought the chapter of my life where I studied the stars was over. What I learned was studying the stars was more than just a chapter. Pretty soon I was star-gazing again as a hobby. That's when I discovered Betty."

No, Betty is not a woman and Betty is not a star. Betty is the code name Dr. Townsend penned for a defunct satellite that he began tracking every night. "Betty started out as sort of a game," Dr. Townsend noted, "but when she became potentially dangerous, I knew I couldn't sit on this information any longer." Dr. Townsend realized that Betty was headed right into the projected path of a space shuttle's upcoming launch. If the shuttle launch was not postponed, there would be a ten-to-one chance the satellite would scratch the heat shield of the shuttle and destroy it, causing the shuttle to burn up as it entered space.

Dr. Townsend called on the most talented and meticulous astronomer he knew—an old co-worker at the MIT labs—Miss Sapphire Pierce. "If there was one person who could keep my secret safe it was Sapphire. We'd collaborated before on several projects and theories. She's smart as a whip. And funny too." The one problem? Dr. Townsend wasn't sure whether or not he could convince his one-time partner to venture out of the house. "I was confident, though. I had a feeling that once Sapphire learned the gravity of the situation she would cave. And I was right."

"It wasn't just Peaker who convinced me," Sapphire added. "It was the confidence of my close friends . . . especially one fellow star-gazer. I knew it was important to be brave and do what I loved. And I knew I could do it."

Miss Pierce and Dr. Townsend worked around the clock for a week until they had enough material to present to NASA. Since then, it has been one great adventure after another for these one-time retirees. Not only did Dr. Townsend and Miss Pierce save the lives of all the astronauts on the shuttle, but they were invited to the White House to accept a special medal for their bravery and pursuit of truth. What's next for these two? Miss Pierce responded, "I don't know . . . and I'm starting to think that's the fun part."

❧ . . . . ❧

"Well, who woulda thunk it!" Mr. Ramsey exclaimed, thunderstruck. "Miss Pierce is a genuine hero!"

"Miss Pierce *is* a real hero!" Charlotte agreed with her father, awestruck at this development. "Imagine . . . she hasn't been out of the house in years, and now she's telling NASA how to fix its mistakes—and then meeting with the *President*! I can't wait to tell her how proud I am of her!" She leaned over to read another article on the front page, one about Miss Pierce herself and her life here in Brookline.

Her father glanced out the window. "Well, I have a feeling you'll be able to do that sooner than you think. Look out there!"

Charlotte turned away from the computer and followed her father's gaze out the window. A long black car slowed to a stop in front of their house, and out stepped

Miss Pierce, looking a little flushed and tired, but otherwise smiling!

Immediately surrounding her were serious-faced men in black suits and dark glasses, and swarming all over the lawn were reporters with cameras and microphones!

"Oh, boy!" Charlotte whispered to her father. "This is the kind of thing Maeve would love, but how do you think Miss Pierce will handle it? She looks overwhelmed."

Just then, Yuri came running up the street, bags of apples in both hands. He must have seen the car pass his stand, because he went straight for the yellow Victorian, dropped the bags on the lawn, pushed his way through the hovering reporters, and wrapped Miss Pierce in a big bear hug, twirling her around.

Charlotte and her dad looked at each other and burst out laughing. Never in a million years would they have predicted the scene in front of them—little Miss Pierce being hugged by the big burly Russian grocer. When Yuri stopped hugging Miss Pierce, Miss Pierce turned even pinker, then threw her arms around Yuri, and hugged him back! A wide-eyed Charlotte wondered, *Could it really be true—is there something going on between Miss Pierce and Yuri?"*

"I better go tell the BSG," Charlotte told her father when they both stopped laughing. "I know they'll be relieved that Miss Pierce is home."

skywriter: OMG, you guys!
Miss Pierce is BACK!!!
4kicks: where was she??
skywriter: DC! she and her
friend saved a space shuttle
from crashing and now she's
famous. reporters r on my
lawn right now . . . everywhere. turn on your tvs.
you'll c
flikchic: no way!!! can I
come over, Char? I'm ready 4
my close-up. I can be there
in 5 minutes!
Kgirl: what r u gonna say if
they ask you about stars and
rockets?
flikchic: just so happens I
know TONS about stars . . .
cary grant, grace kelly, tom
hanks
lafrida: 2 bad u can't study
those kind of stars in science :)
flikchic: I KNOW!!!
skywriter: check out the
Boston Globe website . . .
it explains everything
Kgirl: whoa that is 2 crazy,

6 people here
skywriter
Kgirl
4kicks
flikchic
lafrida
fitzharvard

File Edit People View Help

char. I want to ask grandma
ruby bout this. I wonder if
she knows anything? maybe
she's in on the secret!
4kicks: space debris, huh?
hard 2 believe that old
trash in the universe can
rip open rockets!
skywriter: I know! I guess
people have to b more careful when they put garbage in
the universe
lafrida: NO KIDDING
4kicks: pun intended???
lafrida: YES . . . LOL
fitzharvard: hello?
Kgirl: hey, betsy . . .
fitzharvard: how r u girls?
skywriter: gr8! how r u?
fitzharvard: good. I have a
question 4 u all
flikchic: what's up?
fitzharvard: well u know how
this Spirit Week dance is
falling apart?
4kicks: I think it fell
apart a long time ago
lafrida: seriously
fitzharvard: I have a plan,

6 people here

skywriter
Kgirl
4kicks
flikchic
lafrida
fitzharvard

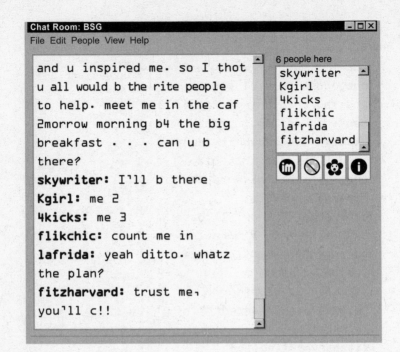

and u inspired me. so I thot
u all would b the rite people
to help. meet me in the caf
2morrow morning b4 the big
breakfast . . . can u b
there?
skywriter: I'll b there
Kgirl: me 2
4kicks: me 3
flikchic: count me in
lafrida: yeah ditto. whatz
the plan?
fitzharvard: trust me,
you'll c!!

20

Stand Up for Spirit

At the Spirit Week breakfast the next morning, Betsy explained to the BSG her new idea to save the school dance. Encouraged by their interested faces, Betsy pulled out a notebook filled with ideas. Avery faked a coughing fit to cover up her laughter when she saw it. It was such typical Betsy stuff—lists and more lists!

"Is this what you were talking about online last night," Maeve asked her immediately, "about us inspiring you?"

"Yes!" Betsy declared, looking at each of them in turn. "I really had an epiphany!" To no one in particular, she explained, "It's kind of a flash-of-light moment—like the heavens opening up—and suddenly you recognize something important."

"Gee, thanks, Betsy." Avery winced. The BSG could hear the sarcasm in her voice, but Betsy completely missed it. Charlotte figured Betsy didn't really mean to be obnoxious. It was just her annoying way of having to share every bit of knowledge she had acquired in her lifetime with those around her.

"Avery." She nodded at Avery first, who smiled back at her. "You had such a great attitude during Sports Day, when the boys were just ruining everything. And Maeve, you kept campaigning for the Birdland theme for the dance even when everybody else shouted you down." Maeve turned pink, but she also smiled. "But most of all I learned what dignity really means from Isabel, who kept her head up and behaved really admirably when everyone was saying mean things that weren't even true." Isabel dropped her eyes, but after all the rotten things that had happened that week, Betsy's praise *did* feel good.

"Charlotte," Betsy went on. Avery squirmed in her seat. Why was Betsy so wordy? Even though what she was saying was pretty nice, it was getting annoying. She wanted Betsy to get to the point already. Avery opened her mouth, only to have Katani kick her under the table.

". . . Charlotte, you kept on asking people what gave them spirit, which was the most important question we all should've been asking this week—and most of us didn't." Charlotte felt warm inside. It felt great to know that someone appreciated her. *Too bad Betsy isn't the editor of the* Sentinel, she thought.

"And Katani," Betsy continued, "who gave the best speech anybody gave this week. Well, except for her sister Kelley." They all laughed. Betsy looked earnestly at Katani. "All last night, I was thinking about how you captured everyone's attention and came up with a plan for fixing the gossip situation, which had gotten way out of hand."

Katani sat up taller. It felt kind of cool to have inspired one of the smartest kids in school, even if she was kind of a know-it-all.

"Thanks for all the nice comments, Betsy, but could you get to the point now?" Avery pleaded. She was ready to do cartwheels around the room.

"Okay." Betsy cleared her throat. "I really don't know how many people in our class could actually organize something as big as a dance, especially in such a hurry. So it's good that I'm here to do it." The BSG sighed. Betsy was *still* Betsy.

Katani agreed with Avery. It was time to get down to business. "So what's the deal on the dance?" she asked in her most businesslike tone. "The clock's ticking here, Betsy."

Betsy nodded. "Right." She opened her notebook. "Well, we all learned this week that spirit is not about winning and losing. It's about what gets you excited and involved. And I think we should keep our theme really simple, so we can use the little time we have left to make it work. How do you feel about "Got Spirit"? as the dance theme?"

"I love that," Katani said at once, and the others nodded enthusiastically.

"It's a classic!" "That is way cool." "It's just what we needed all along!" Everyone was talking at once.

"But, Betsy," Katani hesitated, glancing at the notes in the A+ student's notebook, "how are we going to get this together in time?"

"That's the beauty of it," Betsy answered. "It takes

spirit to make spirit, right? If each person in school just brings one thing to the dance—a poster, a knickknack, a piece of music, whatever they want as a decoration—we'll have *everyone* contributing to the theme, not just a dance committee, and kids will feel excited about being there. And we won't have to worry about organizing the decorations ourselves at the last minute. Don't you think it's a great idea?"

"Betsy, I've got to hand it to you. This is genius," Katani announced. "I can't see how anyone wouldn't love this idea, and we won't have that much to do except tell people about it, because they're going to be the ones bringing in the stuff we need to make the gym look great!"

"That's what I thought," Betsy agreed, looking pleased.

By then the cafeteria was getting more and more crowded, filling up with students who had come for the free breakfast buffet. It was getting so noisy the girls could hardly hear themselves think. Charlotte's distracted glance around the room settled on Kevin and Chase at an all-boy table nearby.

"You know," she said to no one in particular, "I don't think we can pull this off unless we get everyone's cooperation, and there hasn't been a lot of that this week. Don't you think we'd better ask the boys what they think?"

The girls looked over at the boys' table. Chase apparently had recovered from Ms. R's remarks the day before, because he was being as obnoxious and loud as usual. The girls let out a collective sigh. "Well," Betsy paused. "I'm not exactly friends with any of them. Could one of you girls do it?"

The BSG looked at each other. Then everyone turned and looked at Maeve.

"What?" Maeve asked. "Why are you looking at *moi*?"

"Everyone likes you, Maeve," Katani pointed out. "You're good friends with Riley and Dillon, and you can make anyone listen to you. C'mon, girl, harness your spirit!" Her voice rose as she pumped her fist.

Maeve giggled. Katani could be so funny sometimes. But she looked around at her grinning friends. Maybe she *was* the woman for the job. So, she picked up her empty glass and a spoon, hopped on the bench, and stood up on the table. "Attention! *Attenzione!* Everybody!" She tapped with the spoon on the empty glass, like she'd seen people do in the movies. It had the same magical effect now. The boys quieted down and looked up at her.

"Thanks, guys," she said, sounding totally confident. "We've been talking here about putting on the dance, and we think it's not too late to do it with style, if everybody agrees to cooperate."

"Oh, boy." Chase rolled his eyes. "Here it comes . . . Birdland again, from the redheaded *birdbrain*."

Maeve flushed, but she was glad to see that none of the other boys laughed, and Kevin elbowed Chase hard in the ribs. Chase glared at Kevin, but he quieted down after that. "Go ahead, Maeve. Don't listen to this loudmouth," Kevin called out to Maeve.

"No," Maeve went on, as if Chase hadn't rudely interrupted, "it's way too late to do something as sophisticated as Birdland or Under the Sea."

You go girl, Katani silently cheered her friend.

"But listen," Maeve went on. "Spirit Week is about spirit, and spirit is about what moves *each* of us." She went on to explain the idea of having everyone contribute to the decorations in the gym by bringing his or her own personal spirit object. In a few minutes, she was surprised to see that most of the boys were starting to look genuinely excited.

"I don't see why we still can't do the shark thing," Chase began, but to everyone's surprise, Kevin spoke up now, loud and clear.

"Sharks are lame, dude! They're for the *birds*! And I for one am sick of hearing about sharks! I think this idea is too cool, and I even know exactly what I'm going to bring in for the dance. What about you?"

"Oh, so you *got spirit*, do you, Kev?" Chase jeered, obviously feeling upset because his buddy was going along with the girls. "Well, I think spirit is just another word for *girl drama* . . . and I'm sick of it!"

"Dude, you're the one causing all the drama," Kevin fumed. "If it wasn't for you, none of this stuff would've happened!" That brought the biggest laugh of the day, to Chase's embarrassment. The Chase Finley drama was so over.

"So we're agreed, everybody—the theme is Got Spirit?" asked Maeve as she looked around the cafeteria.

"Yeah!" roared the boys. "Great idea, Maeve!"

"Thanks, but this wasn't my idea." Maeve looked over and beckoned Betsy onto the table. With a big "Ta-da!" she presented the embarrassed girl to her classmates. Everyone gave Betsy a well-deserved round of applause, which made Betsy turn the color of a big garden tomato.

CHAPTER

21

Birds of a Feather

K atani looked at her watch for the third time. "Where is that girl? We did say seven o'clock, right? Not seven-thirty?"

Isabel pulled her coat closer around her. "Avery's not usually late. I'm sure there's a good reason." But she was worried. It was time to get going to the Spirit Dance.

"Yeah," Maeve agreed. She had twisted her red curls and pinned them artfully on top of her head, and she wore sparkly dangling green earrings that rested above her coat collar. "Maybe she couldn't decide which team jersey to wear." Avery refused to dress up most of the time, but she did have her own sporty style.

"Somehow I don't think that's it," said Charlotte in a strange voice. She was looking toward the street, and the rest of the BSG swung around to follow her gaze.

There was Avery. Only it wasn't Avery! This girl was wearing jeans, like Avery would, and sneakers—that was right, too. But the sparkly yellow jersey peeking out

❀ 223 ❀

from under her coat was definitely different, and . . . was that a matching yellow headband holding back her soft, smooth—yikes!—*blown-dry* hair?

"Avery?" Isabel asked.

"We seem to have a missing person here," said Maeve in a tough-cop voice. "You there in the fabulous outfit– what do you know about Avery Koh Madden's where- abouts?" Avery couldn't help but crack up.

"Okay, okay! Chill. My mom kidnapped me after school today. She made me go to the hairdresser and bought me a new outfit. Please don't make a big deal out of it."

"Don't make a big deal out of what?" Katani asked. "Oh . . . you mean, like the fact that you look *fantastic*? That's what we're not supposed to make a big deal out of? Okay, no problem!"

"You really do look amazing," Charlotte assured her friend.

"You trying to look amazing for anyone in particular?" Maeve asked mischievously.

"Maeve . . ." Avery warned.

"Hey, just kidding!" Maeve said with an exaggerated expression of innocence on her face.

"And this," Avery shot back, "is a *no joke zone*."

"Whoa! Sorry." Maeve held up her hands.

Katani grinned. "See? That no joke zone thing really does work!"

"Hello, girls." The BSG turned and saw Mrs. Weiss, the owner of Irving's Toy & Card Shop, who was closing up the shop for the evening.

"Hi, Mrs. Weiss!" they all returned the greeting. Ethel

Weiss always had kind words and great advice for the kids who frequented her store.

"You all look very lovely this evening. Where are you off to?"

"We're going to our Spirit Week school dance," Maeve answered.

"Oh, is it that time of year again?" Mrs. Weiss smiled at the BSG as she glanced at their outfits. "We dressed a little differently in my day, but I was just as excited as you girls are for a chance to dance with some handsome young men."

"Handsome young men?" Avery made a gagging noise.

Mrs. Weiss chuckled. "Well, have a wonderful time tonight. Come by for some Swedish fish tomorrow and tell me all about it!"

"We will!" the BSG promised and waved to Mrs. Weiss as they started toward the school.

The BSG were all eager to see the gym transformed, but when they walked in, they were stunned. The decorations weren't exactly beautiful, but they were *powerful*. Everyone had brought in his or her favorite spirit symbol, and the gym radiated excitement. Posters were hung everywhere, and stuffed animals and little statuettes decorated long tables of refreshments. Buttons and pins were stuck on cork boards, which had been mounted on the walls. The bright, bold colors lifted everyone's spirits, and if things were hung a little haphazardly and hastily, no one seemed to care. Betsy had been right. Seeing everyone's contribution was truly uplifting!

Riley sat behind a long table stacked with audio equipment; he was acting as DJ for the dance. "Okay, BSG, I've got things to do. Catch you all later," Avery quipped, and then disappeared into the crowd. Two minutes later the girls saw her walk up to Dillon, punch him lightly in the arm, and start a conversation.

"Ha-ha, look at that!" Maeve giggled. "Dillon didn't even recognize Avery at first!"

"Thanks for sticking up for the girls, dude," Avery said to Dillon. "It was a cool thing to do."

Dillon shrugged, but he kept looking at her yellow headband and jersey and different hair, as though wondering where his old sports buddy Avery went. "Hey, no problem. Some of the guys acted like real jerks, including me. . . ."

"Hey, you guys just can't help yourselves," Avery said, and they both laughed. Then she added, "Want to dance? I mean, as long as you promise not to throw me up in the air like a human football."

Dillon looked happy that the awkwardness was over between them. "Yeah, good idea," he agreed.

At Maeve's request, Riley was mixing it up at his DJ post with some top hits as well as some old stuff from the Birdland era. Five minutes later, Avery and Dillon were flying across the floor to one of the fast, jazzy songs. Dillon did a quick feet-first turn, and caught Avery's hands as she did the same thing, even faster. "Hey, you're really good! I didn't know you could dance like that! I thought you hated to dance!"

Avery gave him a condescending look. "Oh, please . . . like coordination and grace are only important on the athletic field? That stuff sticks with you on the dance floor too, you know. Plus, it's fun exercise."

"I guess," Dillon said, watching Avery execute another quick turn and then a moonwalk-type backward shuffle. "And where'd you learn that? I don't think they have a move like that in soccer or basketball!"

"Nope," Avery said with a grin. "But I also happen to have the services of a great private dance tutor . . . the one, the only, Maeve Kaplan-Taylor!"

The rest of the BSG hadn't started dancing yet. They were hanging out at the snack table when suddenly Katani felt a tug on her sleeve. It was Kelley, looking super-excited and happy. "Katani, come on! I need you—now! Now, now, now, now, NOW!"

She grabbed Katani's off-the-shoulder sweater and dragged her toward the dance floor, where a tall, handsome boy was waiting. Katani knew, looking up at him, that she'd never met him before. "Katani, this is Miguel," Kelley said proudly to her sister. "Miguel is my friend in activities. He wanted to meet you . . . very, very much. He said he wanted to *formally* meet you. Formally, formally."

Katani could see where this was going. "Thanks, Kelley. Can you get some punch for me?"

Kelley stared at her sister. "Punch, punch, a bunch of punch." She laughed and said, "No!" But at least she had stopped her song.

Miguel lowered his eyes and shoved his hands in his pockets, but Katani pretended not to notice and stuck out her hand. Anyone who had been nice to Kelley was somebody she wanted to meet. "Hi. It's nice to meet you." Relieved, Miguel smiled and offered his hand.

"I'm going back to listen to the music," Kelley told Katani. "Formally, formally . . ."

She ran off, unconcerned about Katani and Miguel. Miguel managed to shake Katani's hand back. "Kelley's a great girl," he said. "And she's always talking about you."

Katani looked up at him, trying to figure out how to ask the question that sprang into her mind: Was Miguel in Kelley's class?

Miguel saw her confusion and explained, "Oh, I'm on the eighth-grade community service team. We help out in Kelley's class sometimes. That's how she knows me."

Ah, Katani thought. And all this time she'd thought the guy that Kelley kept talking about was one of her classmates! "She talks about you a lot too," Katani said out loud. "I just didn't realize . . . I thought you were . . . you know, actually in her class." But then they both laughed, so it was all right. Miguel was very cute. Katani suddenly had an urge to smooth her hair, which she resisted.

"I saw your speech yesterday," Miguel went on, seeming more relaxed. "And I thought it was really great. I told Kelley I wanted to say hello to you to let you know that. But I didn't mean for her to drag you away from your friends . . ."

"That's okay," Katani answered, glancing back over her shoulder at the BSG. Maeve grinned and waved at her. Katani smiled. Maeve had obviously recovered from her Birdland disappointment.

"Well, as long as we're here . . . would you like to dance?" Miguel asked.

"Sure," Katani answered as her heart skipped a beat. The two of them moved off onto the crowded floor.

"C'mon, let's dance," Maeve begged Isabel and Charlotte.

"To this? I don't think I know how to dance to this." Charlotte listened to the old-school disco beat.

"It's a line dance, like from *Saturday Night Fever*," Maeve answered. "It's fine. Come *on!*" She pulled them onto the floor, and in a minute they were all dancing to "Stayin' Alive" as though they'd done it all their lives.

Isabel was beginning to feel pretty good about her dance moves, when she felt a tap on her shoulder. Turning, she saw Kevin standing at her side. "Hey, I know you're dancing," he said a little awkwardly, "but I was wondering . . . Could we talk when you have a minute?"

Isabel glanced at Maeve, who was dancing with her eyes closed, in a world of her own. Charlotte was bopping along beside her and seemed happy enough. "Well, okay," she said. "How about now?"

"Great!" Kevin seemed relieved. "Come on, let's go near the bleachers." He led her to an area of the gym that was very quiet and almost empty.

Isabel had been waiting for the chance to speak to Kevin for a long time. She spoke quickly before she could lose her nerve. "You know, Kevin, I never said anything about you and Amanda. I wasn't the one spreading rumors. I would never do anything like that."

"I know that now," Kevin told her. "It's weird how fast someone can start a rumor and it can just grow. . . ." He shook his head from side to side, his brown hair falling onto his forehead. "This gossip thing is really sick. People get a hold of something, then a few people repeat it, and it doesn't even sound the same as it was the first time. It's even worse on the Internet because you don't see people face-to-face. It's like that old game Telephone. You say to someone, 'I like red cherries' and at the other end it comes out, 'I saw Kevin with a girl named Sherry.'"

"That's exactly right!" Isabel agreed, smiling in relief.

"I think that's why Chase thought he could joke about it," Kevin went on. "Because it wasn't face-to-face when he was online . . . but it was still wrong. The more he said, the more lame it got."

"To me it felt downright mean," Isabel said.

"I'm really sorry," Kevin told her. "It's been hard . . . well, since we talked in the art room, before all that drama with Amanda."

"Is it really just drama?" Isabel looked up at him directly. She thought she'd better ask the question straight out and be sure of what was going on.

"Amanda and I were always better as friends," Kevin admitted. "And one day I think we'll be friends again, but there's nothing else going on between us . . . no matter *what* you hear!" he joked. "When you want to know what's happening with me, just ask me. I'll tell you."

"You will?"

"Yeah. I tell my friends lots of things," Kevin said. "Well, first let's dance. That is, if you're okay being friends with me after everything that's gone down this week."

Isabel looked down for a moment, then up at him with a bright smile. "Yes. Friends. But if I dance with you—" She hesitated.

"What?" Kevin asked.

"Well, people might start talking about us again. And I

hated being talked about all over school and online this week."

"My mom says people are always going to talk," Kevin advised her. "But we don't have to get involved in it. And I'm not going to stop doing something I really want to do because of it."

Isabel took a deep breath and looked at Kevin. "I'd like to dance with you."

Kevin grabbed her hand. "Okay. Let's go for it."

On the way to the center of the floor, Isabel saw Anna and Joline sitting on the bleachers . . . alone. No one, apparently, was interested in dancing with them. She wondered why Chase hadn't asked Anna to dance, but as she looked around she realized she didn't see Chase anywhere and hadn't all night. He must not have come to the dance at all! *Some spirit he has,* she thought. *Lucky we didn't all agree to his silly shark theme!*

Then Isabel caught sight of Henry Yurt moving purposefully toward Anna. It was so hard to figure out, but the Yurtmeister continued to have a first-class crush on Anna, and a chance to dance with her was something he wouldn't miss!

Isabel saw Anna shrug when he spoke to her, but the Queen of Mean tossed her flowing hair over her shoulder, got up and followed him onto the gym floor. Left alone on the bleachers, Joline's face turned dark. Luckily, Pete Wexler sauntered around the corner and asked Joline to dance. With a superior smile plastered on her face, Queen of Mean no. 2 followed Pete onto the floor, making sure that Anna saw her. After all, Pete Wexler was *definitely* cuter than Yurt.

So much for the Queens of Mean, Isabel thought. *I guess good things happen to mean people too!*

She looked around to find her friends. Maeve, of course,

was sitting next to Riley at the DJ booth, listening through a big pair of headphones to some music, and busily picking out tracks for him to play. Isabel wasn't at all surprised when the next song that blared out into the gym was "Summer Nights" from *Grease*—it was one of Maeve's all-time faves!

Charlotte, though, was standing all alone at the punch table. Just as she was wondering how she could convince Kevin, without hurting his feelings, that she had to go spend time with Charlotte, Isabel saw Nick Montoya come around the table holding a punch cup. He offered it to Charlotte with a smile.

"Hey?" Kevin broke into her train of thought. "You look pretty far away. What are you thinking about?"

"Uh–" For a second Isabel was caught completely off guard. Then she thought of something and asked, "I was just wondering what you brought to show your spirit."

Kevin grinned. "It's right over there." And he pointed across the room. "I thought you'd appreciate it."

Isabel turned. Kevin was pointing at the basketball hoop. He thought she'd appreciate *that*? She liked basketball, but she had secretly hoped Kevin would have come up with a way cooler idea.

Suddenly, something hanging in the hoop caught her eye. It was the shimmering bottle-cap fish she'd seen in the art room. "That's your spirit?" she asked, already knowing the answer.

"Yup," Kevin answered his new friend. "Art is my spirit."

To be continued . . .

Just Kidding

BOOK EXTRAS

 Book Club Buzz

 Trivialicious Trivia

 Charlotte's Word Nerd Dictionary

 Keep Safe! Fun Sites for Girls!

Book Club Buzz

10 QUESTIONS FOR YOU AND YOUR FRIENDS TO CHAT ABOUT

1. Spirit Week is a special occasion at Abigail Adams Junior High. Does your school have any big traditions that occur every year? What is the purpose of those traditions?

2. Maeve wants "Birdland." Chase wants "Under the Sea." Betsy Fitzgerald wants "Spirit of Abigail Adams." What would be your fabulous theme for a Spirit Week dance?

3. Kevin is so talented at basketball that not very many people know about his love of art. What are some of your hobbies, passions, or talents that most people probably wouldn't know about?

4. Maeve says that romance always gets in the way of boy/girl friendships, but Avery says that there are plenty of "just

friend" activities that boys and girls can do together. What do you think?

5. Miss Pierce has a favorite quote: "Hitch your wagon to a star." —Ralph Waldo Emerson. What is your favorite quote? If you don't have one, check out a book of quotations!

6. Even though Miss Pierce is the grown-up, sometimes Charlotte feels responsible for her. Do you know anyone who is older than you that you sometimes have to look after? Why?

7. Isabel feels overwhelmed by all the gossip about her. What are some things Isabel could do to regain control of the situation? How could her friends help?

8. Chase Finley's rumor-spreading ways are CERTAINLY not nice. Why do you think Chase behaves like this? If you were Chase's friend, like Kevin, or one of his classmates, what would you tell him?

9. Avery says that her dance outfit is in the "no joke zone." What is in your "no joke zone?"

10. The Internet can be totally awesome, but it is also a place where gossip spreads like wildfire! Why do you think online behavior can get out of line, and what are some things you can do to keep the Internet fun and safe?

Just Kidding trivialicious trivia

1. "Be True to Your School" is a song by what '60s pop group?
   A. The Beatles
   B. The Supremes
   C. The Beach Boys
   D. The Bee Gees

2. What kind of creature is Kevin's art project?
   A. Fish
   B. Human (athletes)
   C. Snake
   D. Bird

3. Who is Harry Wooster's cousin?
   A. Joline Kaminsky
   B. Riley Lee
   C. Betsy Fitzgerald
   D. Kiki Underwood

4. What were the names of the strange-looking outfits—the ones with the ballooning pants—worn by the men in the Birdland clubs?
   A. Count Basie capes
   B. Zoot suits
   C. Puffy pants
   D. Air-filled Jordans

5. One of Miss Pierce's favorite quotes is "Hitch your wagon to a star." What famous historical Massachusetts resident said this?
   A. Henry David Thoreau
   B. Ralph Waldo Emerson
   C. Louisa May Alcott
   D. Benjamin Franklin

6. What did Ms. Pink do to show her spirit during her
   Spirit Week?
   A. She dyed her hair pink
   B. She made pink cupcakes
   C. She ran for chair of the dance committee
   D. She bought La Fanny

7. What extra effort do the girls make to be polite when they
   go to Montoya's?
   A. They never cut in line
   B. They wipe up the milk spills at the counter
   C. They clean up their crumbs and napkins at their table
      when they leave
   D. They buy a pastry for a stranger as a random act of
      kindness

8. Why does Pete Wexler think Avery should not run the
   sports committee?
   A. Because she already has too many extracurricular
      activities
   B. Because she's too short
   C. Because she already ran for class president
   D. Because sports committees are men's work

9. How does Katani hear about the "No Joke Zone?"
   A. From her sister Candice
   B. From Mrs. Fields
   C. From Ethel Weiss
   D. From Ms. Pink

10. How does Avery manage to surprise the BSG before the
dance?
   A. She pulls a practical joke on all of them
   B. She wears her sports gear to show extra spirit
   C. She gets dressed up
   D. She goes to the dance with Pete Wexler

Charlotte Ramsey

Charlotte's Word Nerd Dictionary

BSG Words

Laugh-a-thon: (p. 54) noun—*when you're laughing about something that might not even be that funny, but you still can't stop*

Gidget: (p. 112) noun—*a Yuri word, the same thing as a gadget*

Other Cool Words

Riffling: (p. 1) verb—*to go through in search of something*

Abominably: (p. 1) adverb—*in an offensive or terrible manner*

Disperse: (p. 11) verb—*to spread widely*

Ambitious: (p. 18) adjective—*having a strong desire for success or achievement*

Wingspan: (p. 18) noun—*the distance between the wing tips of an airplane or bird*

Iridescent: (p. 19) adjective—*brilliant, lustrous, or colorful*

Emphatically: (p. 27) adverb—*forcefully or insistently*

Plaintively: (p. 31) adverb—*sorrowfully*

Miffed: (p. 33) adjective—*in an irritable mood*

Drone: (p. 36) verb—*to go on and on in a monotonous voice*

Frenetic: (p. 40) adjective—*frantic or frenzied*

Methodical: (p. 75) adjective—*orderly*

Inconsolable: (p. 77) adjective—*incapable of being comforted*

Humdinger: (p. 85) noun—*something of a remarkable or puzzling effect*

Rambling: (p. 105) adjective—*roaming, sprawling, or wandering*

Boisterously: (p. 109) adverb—*loudly and noisily*

Conspiratorially: (p. 111) adverb—*with the manner of believing there is a larger plot at play*

Exuberant: (p. 141) adjective—*full of enthusiasm or joy*

Unnerved: (p. 145) adjective—*nervous or anxious*

Salvage: (p. 209) verb—*to save from loss or destruction*

Definitions adapted from *Webster's Dictionary*, Fourth Edition, Random House.

Hey girls! We think these websites are really cool !

BEACON STREET GIRLS

The Beacon Street Girls: www.beaconstreetgirls.com
The online center for all things BSG, includes Club BSG, puzzles, games, contests, and tons of fun things to do!

~

Discovery Girls: www.discoverygirls.com
The Discovery Girls website is home to a unique magazine for girls ages 8–12.

~

FactMonster: www.factmonster.com
Fact Monster is a leading reference site that offers kids 8-14 invaluable homework help as well as a wealth of fun facts, games, and quizzes.

~

Funbrain: www.funbrain.com
The Internet's most popular source for games, comics, and online books.

~

KOL: www.kol.com and **RED:** www.bered.com
AOL's websites for kids 6–12 (KOL) and teens 13–17 (RED), KOL and RED offer games, celebrity news, fashion, and educational resources.

~

Yahoo! Kids: kids.yahoo.com
Yahoo! Kids is one of the top destinations for online entertainment including movie trailers, cartoons, and popular kids' characters.

Have fun online . . . Keep safe!

BEACON STREET GIRLS®

Enter to win a trip to

JAMAICA

for you and your family at
www.beaconstreetgirls.com

5 day/4 night trip courtesy of

airJamaica VACATIONS®
The Finest Vacation Service in the World™

SUNSET JAMAICA GRANDE
RESORT & SPA
Ocho Rios

Share the Next

Collect all the BSG books today!

Also . . . Our Special Adventure Series:

Tell your BFFs to meet you on Beacon Street!

Join the Tower Club at **BeaconStreetGirls.com** for Super-cool virtual sleepovers and parties! Personalize your locker and get $5.00 to spend on Club BSG gifts with this secret code

To get your $5 in MARTY☆MONEY (one per person) go to www.BeaconStreetGirls.com/redeem and follow the instructions, while supplies last.